TWO WAYS TO MURDER

A ghostly apparition, a terrified girl, a superstition, and the mystery surrounding a man who had been buried in a barley field near an old castle are the concomitants in a double murder. Allied to them is a strange story of robbery directed by a boss whose men did not know him and had never seen him. It took weeks of detection by Commander Doctor Manson and the Yard's Homicide Squad to discover the truth.

Books by E. & M. A. Radford
in the Linford Mystery Library:

MURDER MAGNIFIED

E. & M. A. RADFORD

TWO WAYS TO MURDER

Complete and Unabridged

LINFORD
Leicester

First published in Great Britain in 1969 by
Robert Hale Limited
London

First Linford Edition
published May 1995
by arrangement with
Robert Hale Limited
London

British Library CIP Data

Radford, E. & M. A.
    Two ways to murder.—Large print ed.—
Linford mystery library
I. Title II. Radford, Mona Augusta
III. Series
823.914 [F]

ISBN 0–7089–7711–1

Published by
F. A. Thorpe (Publishing) Ltd.
Anstey, Leicestershire
Set by Words & Graphics Ltd.
Anstey, Leicestershire
Printed and bound in Great Britain by
T. J. Press (Padstow) Ltd., Padstow, Cornwall

This book is printed on acid-free paper

1

THE great house had stood solid and stately for some 300 years overlooking the Downland village — or hamlet as some called it — of Taceham. Around it on all sides spread an estate, the ground of which was older even than the house.

Lawns trodden by countless feet over the centuries shelved to a meeting point at a lake of calm water on which ducks and moorhens paddled lazily. Doves cooed in the leafy tops of ancient oaks and elms, and pigeons strutted along the paved terraces. Quietude surrounded the rural picture: and peace, not yet dispelled by tragedy, and murder.

Commander William Bowman standing in the shade of the pillared entrance to the house, gazed outwards at the occupied garden seats round the lakeside. He stepped forward, turned, and with his back to the water, looked upwards at the grey stone of his house. Oddly, it had not the air of coldness so often accompanying houses of unadorned greyness and built of hard granite; centuries of sun and rain, of warmth and chill seemed to have impregnated it with a pleasant mellowness.

Bowman was the owner. A tall man, somewhat aloof though a good mixer when men — and women — from cultivation of his society got to know him well. He carried his six feet-plus easily underneath red hair and a nose that has the shape common only to two races — the Jew and the Norman.

A house had stood on the site in Saxon days when a *ton* fell around it (a *ton* in those days meant what we today call a farm or an enclosure).

Not so imposing a house as the present; but one built of rough flint and lath and wattle.

That was before Herleva, daughter of a humble tanner of Falaise, made a mistake and found that Count Richard of Normandy had fathered a bastard upon her. Thirty-eight years later, that same bastard, named William, heading some ten thousand men, appeared in a fleet of small ships off shore at Pevensey, in Sussex. The ten thousand came ashore armed to the teeth. To the affrighted villagers William gave an assurance. "Good people all," he roared, "We come for your good, for all your goods." He was not conversant with our language, especially with the plurals of it; which explains why one wit, standing by, remarked, "he should have added 'and chattels'." The remark, fortunately, William did not overhear; but the prophecy came true; William the Conqueror did, indeed, very soon have all our chattels!

The invading army threw up *mottes* and earthwork defences on the beach, marched upon the town of Pevensey, passed on. A fortnight later they occupied the town of Hastings after a show of strength at a place since called Battle. After slaying a king of England, William assumed his crown.

And that is where this story had its beginnings. With the crown safely on his head, William handed out rewards to his captains — from the lands of Sussex filched from owners who had held them for generations. To his captain, Roger de Montgomery, went that part of the county known as Arundel. Captain William de Braose became lord of the manor of Brembre, well inland. Both he and Roger de Montgomery were under the return obligation to build solid castles to overlook and guard the conquered countryside. The castle of Arundel still stands through numerous changes of ownership; but all that remains of the castle of Brembre (now called Bramber) are a few stones piled one on another, high up the grassy Downs.

William de Warrenne, son-in-law of the Conqueror, became overlord of Lewes, and Robert Count of Mortain (half-brother) of the lands inland from there. There was one more captain who shared in the Sussex handout, John de Petitoeil, captain of William's crossbow archers. He and his men shot the way from Pevensey to Hastings. If Harold did, indeed, die from an arrow through an eye — as has been said — then it is likely that John de Petitoeil shot it: for only a captain or one of higher rank — could shoot at a king. It was probably for this shot that William put John de Petitoeil in charge of a company of bowmen to hold the Sussex roads clear of enemies, and to shoot down insurrection John stationed himself at Taceham. He seized all the lands, evicted the family from the lath and wattle house, and built in its place a mansion, reared a family, and founded a dynasty.

The yokels, serfs and villeins failed to get their tongues round the word Petitoeil (it meant 'little eye'); they called him by the job they knew only too well that he did — they named him Bowman.

The nickname persisted . . . became a surname, as did so many occupations over centuries. Since then a Bowman had always occupied the great house. Not the original house of John de Petitoeil: that had been destroyed in the Civil War of 1642. But a Bowman had rebuilt it, with nearly the same stones, and had restored over the doorway the original crest carved in stone — a crossbow with an arrow stretched ready to leave it.

These were the thoughts of William Bowman as, back to the lake, he looked up at Saxon Hall Hotel — for that is what John de Petitoeil's mansion had become. Into his mind came the old tag, *sic transit gloria mundi*. Death duties over three generations, coupled with taxation, had reduced the ancient family to 'trade'. His only consolation was that Saxon Hall was a very exclusive hotel; its advertisements were in only the Society journals and the glossy magazines. They ran: 'enjoy a "Country House" holiday'.

A country house it had really become, luxurious and expensive, with pile carpeting throughout, a billiards-room with two tables, a library of more than two thousand books, three large lounges, one with club arm-chairs, a ladies' drawing-room, a bar — and a *cordon bleu chef*. The hotel ran a valet and ladies' maid service.

Accepted guests were in the same luxury class. Should they want to ride, there were horses; should they fish, private waters were available; golf was a quarter-of-a-mile away. Thus it was that Saxon Hall was always full of desirables. Bowman was, in fact, himself regarded by his guests as a social desirable by reason of his ancient lineage.

The Commander's reverie at this precise moment in the story was interrupted by his head gardener and groundsman, Silas Markham. "Guv'nor," he said, "there's a ruddy great car takin' up three parkin' places. We'll need 'em for the week-end. Is the gennelman a'stayin' 'ere and will you ask him to move the car so as the perishin' bonnet is pointin' innards 'stead of bein' broadside on?"

"What car is it, Markham?"

"A ruddy great Oldsmobile."

Bowman walked with his groundsman to the parking place at the rear of the hotel. He stared with ruffled brows at the car, dirty and rusty in places, with a hanging wing and battered rear. "Good god, Markham," he said, "there's nobody staying in the hotel with a bus like that. Wouldn't have it in the place, nor the owner of it."

"Well, its here, sir, and this is our private parkin' place."

"When did it come?"

"Search me, sir. It's bin here, I knows, sin' Tuesday but I ain't worried abaht it until now when we'll be wantin' parkin' space."

"Shove the damned thing in among the trees. We don't want it seen in the open."

In the hotel the Commander wore

a worried look. He knew most of the people who stayed in the hotel, or came on a visit, and knew, too, the make of cars they drove. He could recall none who drove a ramshackle Oldsmobile of an age which he put at fifteen years. Mulling over it with a glass of sherry he wondered whether it might have been driven by a man who stayed for lunch and dinner with a Mr. and Mrs. Worth. There had been no other strangers outside him to his knowledge who had accompanied guests in the hotel.

Pouring out a second glass of sherry he slouched back in his chair and frowned at the accoutrements of his office: the Cambridge oar he had earned in the 1920 Boat Race, which now hung lengthwise over the mantelpiece; the golfing cup brought back from Hoylake which stared out of a glass case on the sideboard; sporting knick-knacks rubbing silver alongside filled photo frames. The room was permeated with his personality: and with the fragrance that comes from the smoke of good cigars. That car had him considerably worried.

A telephone call was to deepen the worry. "Yes?" he called into the inter-com. "Markham here, sir," the gardener's voice explained. "We've shoved that car back in the trees, like you said." There was a pause.

"Well," Bowman said, "have you found out anything about the owner?"

"No, sir, but there's one thing you ought to know . . . " Markham paused.

"All right, come on, man, unless it's a dark secret. What is it?"

"The engine, sir. It's bin hotted up — doctored. I reckons it could do well over a hunerd miles an hour."

"The devil!"

"An' the seats is hollow, if you gets me meaning. Made to hide things. I reckons as the police ought ter know."

"All right, Markham. I'll think over what to do about it."

"Suppose, sir, the owner comes in and drives off without our knowing, as you might say. Us wants to know for why he left it there."

"H'm, that's a point. We want to see the bounder." He thought for a moment, and then came to a decision. "We've got some chains in the garage, haven't we? Well, thread them through each of the wheels and padlock them. There are padlocks in the garage. Then bring me the keys. The car can't be moved while the wheels are chain-locked."

Bowman returned to his immediate problem. The only person he could see who could have driven down was the guest of the Worths. The family were special clients, visiting the hotel and staying two or three days every month. Worth himself was a financier with a number of influential friends. He did not want to offend them by criticising the conduct of the man who had spent a day in the hotel with them. Should he be a close friend they might take umbrage; it was nothing to do with them if the man left his car in the park.

Saxon Hall was open to non-residents for meals or a drink and there were people, seeing the fact publicised on a board at the entrance to the drive, who came in for either of those purposes. The car might have been owned by one of them. But, if so, why on earth did they leave it and go home on their feet? Forgotten that they had come by car? Nonsense! There were no places within walking distance of the hotel except the homes of the villagers, and none of them could run cars like the Oldsmobile, aged though it was. However, to make sure he consulted the head waiter. Jose, a Spaniard, was quite emphatic that no stranger had had a meal in the hotel other than the guest of Mr. and Mrs. Worth. The barman was equally emphatic that he had served no drinks to a stranger.

These facts decided Bowman. He felt he had to make sure one way or another. At the reception desk he copied the Worths' London address from the register, asked Telephone

Directory for the number and put through a call. It was answered by Mrs. Worth.

"Mr. Bowman," she said. "How nice to hear from you. We are thinking of coming down this week-end, if you have room for us."

"I can always find a room for you, madam," he assured her, gallantly. "I'll book it right away. Friday to . . . ?"

"Oh, to Tuesday, of course."

"Right-O. By the way you remember that when you were last here you and Mr. Worth had a guest for tea and dinner?"

"Mr. de Frees — yes."

"Do you know whether he drove down?"

"I expect so. Why?"

"Do you know what make of car he drives?"

"Good gracious, no. He's more a friend of my daughter, really."

"Would he be still in the vicinity, do you think?"

"I shouldn't have thought so. He

hates the country anyway, and only came down because of Mary. Why the inquiry?"

"It sounds silly, but we have a car left in the park. It has been there more than a week now and we cannot imagine who can be the owner. Mr. de Frees is the only person we can trace outside our booked guests who might have come down by car."

"Well, I can assure you that Mr. de Frees went back to London the same night. He said that he had an important appointment for early the following morning. He left, I think, about ten o'clock."

"Then that settles that. I'll probably have to contact the police to find the owner. I'm sorry to have troubled you. Be seeing you at the week-end."

2

M RS. WORTH related the incident to her husband when he reached home in the evening. "Very odd," he commented . . . "Very odd indeed."

"He did go back that night, didn't he, dear? You saw him off, did you not?"

"Well, I saw him leave the porch, Ellie. I didn't go outside. It was raining like hell, as you know. But he turned in the direction of the car park." He thought for a moment. "I shouldn't mention it to Mary, anyway. She's in a bad enough way as it is."

"You don't think . . . ?"

"I don't think anything. I didn't like the man and cannot see what Mary sees in him. I made it plain what I thought. Now, let's drop the matter and have dinner."

There were *dessou des cartes* for Worth's warning; and they were associated with the aftermath of the visit Johnny de Frees had paid to Saxon Hall. The Worths and Mary, their only child, had been staying in the Hall for a week when de Frees appeared. Worth had not met him, though he had heard stories about him: and didn't like what he had heard. Mrs Worth had seen him once with her daughter in the street, and though not attracted by him she had, mother-like, suspended judgement.

Since he will figure prominently in the story, a description of him seems necessary. He was a man of about thirty, five feet eight inches tall, but appeared in excess of that by reason of his slimness. One might have called him good-looking in an Italian or Jewish way. A sallow complexion was exaggerated by black hair over-waved and shining with oil: and by his deep-set, black eyes. His dress followed the Carnaby Street fashion with charcoal-grey drain-pipe trousers and a jacket of the same shade. A large diamond ring disfigured the forefinger of his right hand, and an ostentatious Italian watch, gold of course, performed a similar operation on his left wrist. What Mary Worth had seen in him would have presented an absorbing problem to a psychologist. She, herself, possessed a fine figure and glamorous legs, a lot of hair which ought to have been brown but had been lightened. A broad forehead and delicate nose was slightly marred by a wide, thin-lipped mouth, but atoned to some degree by a creamy complexion. She possessed appeal and would, one thought, have been attracted by a more prepossessing man than de Frees.

Mary had taken him direct to the private sitting-room of her parents on his arrival, and introduced him. Tea was served in the room. Conversation over the tea cups was friendly without being exactly cordial. A host, Worth decided, must take his guests as they come.

With the tea tray removed by a maid, he stood up. "Well, de Frees," he announced, "I'll show you over the grounds. They are well worth seeing, and we can have a smoke and a chat."

An embarrassed mother, and an anxious girl worried at the prospect of her father and young man talking where she could not overhear, and interrupt, watched them leave the hotel entrance and start up a steep slope at the top of which lay a herbaceous border, a feature of the hotel grounds and a popular walk for visitors. It is contained in two borders on each side of a wide path of cut grass, and houses some two thousand plants and shrubs, presenting a mass of colour and almost overpowering perfume.

At the far end ornamental iron gates lead the way into a field of barley, ripening golden in the sun. A worn path along the edge of the barley wanders along the crest of the Downs and meanders, did one care to go, to the farm below, and thence to the main road, to Storrington.

The pair returned after half an hour in time for drinks in the cocktail bar before dinner. For the meal they sat a foursome, eyed by glances from guests, intrigued by the incongruity of the appearance between the Worth trio and their guest.

At nine-thirty a violent storm broke over the Downs accompanied by thunder and lightning. Mary Worth, alarmed, suggested that de Frees should stay over the night rather than drive back to London through the storm. De Frees said, however, that he had to be away again in the very early morning on urgent business.

He was accompanied downstairs to the hall by Mary and her father who, as the host, speeded the parting guest. Pulling him aside for a moment Mary quizzed him on the talk with her father, and how it had gone.

"Don't worry," he had said. "Everything will be straightened out, and I will telephone you from London in the morning about one o'clock."

He joined her father in the open door and disappeared through it into the pouring rain. Worth turned away to saunter into the bar for a final night-cap; Mary rejoined her mother in the private room. The atmosphere was a little strained, and after half an hour the girl went up to bed. Mrs. Worth, waiting up until the bar closed had a long talk with her husband; the result was a large measure of disagreement.

★ ★ ★

There had been no call from Johnny de Frees next day at one o'clock, nor at two o'clock. Though an anxious Mary waited near the instrument all through the day and evening no ring came, and when darkness ended the day there was, to quote Foe, only 'silence and desolation, and dim night'.

The following day Mary developed a *malaise* which the absence of news hardly seemed, in the view of her parents, to warrant. Her mother pleaded with her for a little restraint.

"Look, child," she argued. "He told you he had an urgent appointment. You should know from your father what business can do to arrangements. It has probably taken him away and kept him where he is unable to telephone. He's probably written, but you know the state of the postal service these days."

Mary, however, had another view. She knew why Johnny had come to Saxon Hall: and had a good idea of why her father had taken him for the afternoon walk, and had said nothing to her on their return. She bearded her father in the empty library where he had gone for a quiet read.

"You and Johnny talked about us," she said. "I know that. What have you and he arranged about our being married? I want to know."

Worth eyed her in silence for the space of a minute, watching her angry face and her eyes slumbering in wrath, and then spoke quietly. "I did indeed speak to your Johnny," he said. "I don't like him and I don't like what my inquiries about him revealed after your mother had seen and spoken to him in the street. He has no known business connections and no background of family or conduct. I made those facts plain to him. How you, with your upbringing and education, came to be mixed up with him I fail to comprehend. If, as you say, you love this slick two-timing Italian gigolo and want to marry him, that's up to you. I'm warning you that it is the little money you have and the money that will come to you from your grandfather in a year's time that he is after. I have no doubt you have told him about that; he said that you had money of your own. So, you go ahead. I'm saying nothing more except that not one penny of our money will go to you if you bring that man into the family. The matter is now closed so far as I am concerned."

"How do you know he has no business? It was for a business appointment that he drove back to London through the storm, when he could have stayed at the Saxon."

"I know because I have made inquiries, my girl. What do you expect a father would do, when his daughter wants to marry some man he has never heard of? He is a gigolo, living on his wits and on what he can get out of silly women."

"I don't believe it. It's a lie."

"All right, it's a lie — to you."

At ten o'clock Mary gave up her telephone vigil and went to bed. She started to mount the staircase. A minute later her screams brought people tumbling out of the bar and lounges. They brought the head porter and the secretary out of the office.

Mary Worth was lying half-way down the first flight of stairs below the large, square landing. Her screams were now moans, and her left hand was holding on to the staircase staves, which had prevented her falling the full depth of the staircase. The grasp was so tight that the porter had a difficult task to pull her free.

The receptionist and a woman guest carried her, unconscious, to her room and laid her on the bed. The porter rushed downstairs to inform Mr. and Mrs Worth, who had been in the television-room, some distance in the rear of the hotel, and had not heard the screams. Commander Bowman telephoned for a doctor and then went up to the room with a glass of brandy.

It was three-quarters of an hour before Mary could speak intelligently to explain her screaming. When she did so, she told a curious, unbelievable, story. "I was just coming up to the landing," she said, "when I saw a figure in front of the big picture and in front of me. It stretched out its hands towards me and I saw they were covered with blood. I was afraid they'd touch me, so I started back down the stairs. I was terrified. Then I slipped backwards through missing a stair, but managed to grasp at the banisters. I screamed then, and I think I fainted. I don't remember any more."

It was a strange story. Father pooh-poohed it. "Just imagination, Mary," he insisted. "You are upset, of course, through not hearing from that man." Her mother settled her in bed with a warm drink.

Back in the lounge, Mr. and Mrs. Worth heard a different version, even more curious than that of Mary. At the back of the wide landing topping the first flight of stairs, and before the staircase turned at right-angles to the upper regions, there hung a life-size oil painting of a Bowman ancestor of some 300 years ago. Cracked and discoloured by age, the figure was that of a man dressed all in black with white ruffles at his neck and sleeves.

There was a severe expression on his face which was painted, but over the years had faded to whiteness. Over the landing at a height of some ten feet was a large square roof-light with, at the back of it, a pilot light at night to light the turn in the staircase.

"It's an odd thing," Miss Alicia Hall, the receptionist, said to Mr. and Mrs. Worth, over a late brandy in the lounge where they had gathered to recover from the excitement. "It is an odd thing but sometimes, when the pilot light is shining, and by some means is deflected, persons walking up the staircase have seen a figure appear suddenly in front of them. Lots of people have had a temporary shock until they realised, by moving aside, that it is a trick of the light. It's the first time I've heard of blood on the hands, but the background of the picture, behind the man's hands, is dark red very faded with age and the light shining at an angle, helped by the side of the stairs Mary was climbing could well lighten the colour."

On her way to the staff quarters, Miss Hall was intercepted by the porter, Harry Jones. He had the air of a conspirator. "Mark my words, Hall," he whispered in her ear. "Mark me words, that's a warning. He allus gives a warnin', that poor wanderin' soul."

Miss Hall pulled him into the office and closed the door. She, too, whispered, "Keep your ideas to yourself, Jonesy," she said. "It don't do to take a three hundred year old ghost seriously, especially with customers. Some can't take a joke."

"T'ain't no joke, Miss Hall, mum. Three hunerd years agone he killed his daughter wot was goin' to have a baby and her never married, now he tries to warn others of the sex of death a'comin'. He's expiating a sin."

Miss Hall shook her head, angrily. "Well, you keep that to yourself for all our sakes. This is a hotel and if clients think they're going to be haunted by a ghost, it won't do the hotel any good — and it's our living."

Nevertheless, despite her assurances to Jones, Miss Hall was disturbed in mind. It was a fact that there was a legend of ghostly wanderings in the Hall. They had been seen by terrified servants over the years — a young woman wringing her hands was one. The legend here was one of a newly-born baby, illegitimate, which had been killed by being thrown on a fire by the girl's father. A second apparition haunted, it was said, one of the outbuildings — all that remained of the original mansion. It was that of a man wandering round in Norman chain-mail, and carrying a broadsword. It was an addition to both hauntings and legends that each time one or the other was seen, a death followed in the house. A queer thing is superstition.

Next morning, Mary Worth said she wanted to go back home. Her parents thought it best in the circumstances, to humour her, and all three left after lunch in the Bentley. Nothing more had been said of the staircase fall, or of the apparition the girl said she had seen; she had accepted the story of imagination due, she was assured, to worry over the absence of news of Johnny de Frees.

Another sensation, of a lesser sort, was aired at Saxon Hall, after the departure of the Worths. Inspector Ross drove up and parked his car at the rear of the hotel. He walked in and met Bowman.

"Ha, Inspector," the Commander said, "would it be about that blasted car?"

"It would, sir. We've been over it at the station and been in touch with the registration authorities."

"And who is the half-witted owner?"

"We don't know. You see, the registration plates are fakes. There is no such number registered in Sussex, or anywhere else for that matter. Look, sir, are you absolutely sure you have no idea who could have driven the car down here?"

"Absolutely, Inspector. I've gone over it with my staff, and the only person who could possibly have come in it was a friend of the Worths — you've met them — and he went back the same night. Mr. Worth saw him off — and he wasn't walking back to London. We can account for all the other cars." He snorted. "What the hell does a fellow want with a hotted-up car with false plates, and why the devil does he dump it on me, unless . . . "

"Yes, unless what, sir?"

"Unless it was used in a smash-and-grab or a break-in or something and had to be got rid of."

Inspector Ross smiled. "We'd thought of that, sir. The only snag is there are no reports of anything of the kind in which a car was concerned."

"All right, but the car *was* here. Now *you've* got it and the ball is in your court." Commander Bowman washed his hands clear of it, like Pilate of old.

3

WHILE Commander Bowman and Inspector Ross were engaged in verbal combat at Saxon Hall, Mary Worth, back in London, was telephoning for the umpteenth time to Johnny de Frees's flat — and getting no reply. She dialled the number of the caretaker of the block and inquired whether he knew where was Johnny.

"No, miss," he said, and sounded annoyed at the inquiry. "He went off to the country more'n a week ago and I haven't seen him since — No, he didn't say where he was going" — this in answer to her further inquiry — "but he couldn't have reckoned on being away all this time because the milk, bottles and bottles of it, is standing in the service cupboard, and there are groceries as well."

Mary took the news to her father and mother. "You can say what you like," she stormed, "but I want Johnny and I'm going to have him. I don't know what you told him at Saxon Hall. All I know is that I haven't seen him or heard of him since. If you've sent him off, you're going to be sorry for it. I'm going to report his disappearance to the police and ask them to find out where he is."

"If it will give you satisfaction or peace of mind, Mary, I'll have a word with the police myself," Worth said. "They can come here, and you can hear what I say to them."

Detective-Inspector Coleman arrived an hour later, and listened to the story. He joined his fingers in a tent, and thought. Then: "Now look here, sir, and you, Miss, Mr. de Frees is a grown man. He might have gone off on a business trip and found that it has taken him longer than he expected. The fact that he has not cancelled the milk and groceries bears that out. He hasn't been gone long enough to be counted as a missing person, as would be the case if he was a young girl or a child. Tell you what. I will put inquiries into effect to see whether he might have been concerned in an accident anywhere. Have you a photograph of him?" She hadn't, but described him pretty accurately. Outside the front door Worth confirmed and enlarged on the description.

"H'm," Coleman said, "I'm not exactly enamoured by the man, sir."

"Neither am I, Inspector. I had a talk with him and told him that I didn't think he was the man for my daughter. He wasn't too pleased about it."

"Do you think that his not getting into touch with her might be put down to your opposition?"

"No, I do *not*. My girl has considerable means of her own and very good expectations. I would say that the fact would be a magnet to him. He struck me as very much that kind, a gigolo."

"Where did she meet him?"

"That I don't know. She has never confided the fact to us. Candidly, I hope you find no trace of him."

Mary Worth, after the departure of the police officer, appeared to be a little more cheerful in the knowledge that inquiries were to be made officially. Her father noted the fact with satisfaction; but Mrs. Worth, with that maternal instinct all mothers are supposed to possess, nurtured the idea that her daughter's attitude was less one of aggravation at the apparent desertion of de Frees, as of something deeper and far-reaching.

Mary, she reflected, had had boy-friends before and had, indeed, been engaged at one time. Ellie Worth had hopes at one time the girl would marry Oliver Hyams, a lawyer. It would have been in every way an excellent match. But Hyams for some reason had cooled off. Her daughter's demeanour over de Frees, she felt, was at variance with that shown when other affairs had ended, notably that with Hyams. Then, she had shown violent anger followed by violent upbraiding. Now, there was no anger, but a deep-lying qualm to which she had not given verbal expression. The apparent air of cheerfulness, she felt, was pseudo, more of hope than satisfaction. Nevertheless, the girl became more relaxed, and even agreed to an arrangement made to go down to Taceham for a week-end, provided, she said, that the police inspector was given the address in order that he could telephone her if and when he heard anything about Johnny.

They drove down in the Bentley the following afternoon, arriving at Saxon Hall in time for a bath, drink and change before dinner. If the atmosphere brought any reminiscences of the earlier night spent there with de Frees, Mary Worth did not show it. She and her father and mother sat in the large lounge chatting with other guests until after ten o'clock, when Mary went to her room. No hands stretched out to clutch at her as she started up the staircase, and there were no disturbances during the night.

The following (Saturday) morning dawned with the promise of what in meteorological language is referred to as an Indian Summer. Sun shone deeply blue from an unclouded sky, and by ten-thirty o'clock the lawns at Saxon Hall were dotted with men in white flannels, and women in light and gaily-coloured frocks. Half a dozen couples were punting round the lake, to the protests of ducks and other water-fowl intent on finding a meal.

Worth and a visitor from Jersey were playing Pitch-and-Putt golf behind a couple dithering ahead of them on the extensive front lawn. Mrs. Worth and her daughter partnered on a side lawn an elderly man and woman in a croquet challenge. At tables and chairs, shaded by vari-coloured sun umbrellas, waitresses were carrying out 'elevenses' in cooling drinks to assorted guests. The scene emphasised Cowper's

> *Rural sights . . . rural sounds*
> *Exhilarate the spirit, and restore*
> *the tone of languid Nature.*

with birds singing between dips in the elaborate bird-bath standing on the edge of the terrace within view of guests in the lounge. The only discordant note produced was a staccato clatter coming from a tractor operating in the direction of the herbaceous border.

The barley crop had been harvested, and the tractor was ploughing up the ground preparatory to fertilising and the sowing of a winter crop.

With startling suddenness the harsh clatter of the tractor ceased; the abrupt change from staccato to silence appeared alarming to the players. Two minutes later a man came racing down the slope to the hotel front. He was running as though one of the hotel's fabled ghosts was chasing him. As he dashed into the hotel lobby, the arms of the hotel porter obstructed entrance.

"Here, what the hell . . . " the porter began.

"Where's the telephone?"

"You can't come in here like this and take the bloody place over . . . "

"The phone, you ruddy fool. It's urgent. I want the police . . . "

Commander Bowman looked round the door of his office. "What's going on?" he demanded.

"I want to phone . . . police," the intruder said. He crossed to the office door. "Your phone!" he demanded.

"What about, man?"

"Me tractor just turned up a man in the barley field."

Bowman started visibly. "In *my* field . . . a dead man! Who is he?"

"How the hell do I know, sir. I never seed him afore he come up."

"How the devil does he come to be lying in my field?"

"He weren't lying, sir. He wuz buried."

"Buried? . . . Here give me the phone . . . Police," he said . . . "Inspector Ross."

★ ★ ★

The police brought the body down on a stretcher, a difficult task with a load down the steep slope. The hotel guests, gathered in groups, stood ghoul-like as the procession went along the drive to an ambulance drawn up by the gates. As it passed alongside the lawns a ripple of breeze sweeping through a gap in the trees blew the sheet covering the body slightly aside and exposed an arm.

Mary Worth watching with fascinated gaze paid to morbidness, suddenly screamed. The startled carriers jerked to a halt and nearly dropped their burden.

Mary pointed hysterically to a gold watch showing on the uncovered wrist.

"*That's Johnny's watch*," she shouted. "*It's Johnny.*"

Before the nearly paralysed company could stop her she darted forward, pulled back the top part of the sheet and looked at the face beneath.

"*Johnny*," she said, and fainted.

Womenfolk carried her into the hotel and up to her bedroom. A doctor called urgently gave her a sedative injection, and instructions as to how she should be treated when she recovered consciousness. He paid a second visit after lunch when he gave her a thorough examination. Then he made his way to the Worths' private sitting-room.

Mr. and Mrs. Worth rose and waited, anxiety in their glances. The doctor smiled reassuringly. "You have no need to worry," he pronounced, and they eased their tension. "Your daughter has had a very bad shock" — he did not know, not having been told the nature of the shock. "She will be all right in a day or two, but keep her quietly in bed, in her own home if possible. *It shouldn't upset the baby.*"

The latter statement shocked the pair

into momentary silence; but only for a moment. Then the suppressed voice of Mrs. Worth gave tongue. "The baby . . . the baby . . . " she said. "What on earth are you talking about? My daughter is an unmarried woman. Baby indeed!"

Doctor Macrae shuffled uncomfortably in his seat. "I am desolated, Mrs. Worth," he said. "I had no idea that you didn . . . Nevertheless . . . " His voice lapsed into silence; but his eyes sought and held the gaze of Mr. Worth.

"Do you mean, doctor, that Mary is . . . is . . . in . . . ?" his voice broke.

"Two months gone, sir . . . yes, two months." He turned towards the door. "I'll look in on Miss Worth again in the morning." The door closed behind him.

From watching the closing door, the Worths transferred their gaze to each other, incredulity in their faces. They stared for what seemed an age but was no more than half a minute. Then, with full realisation of what the doctor had said, Ellie Worth collapsed on the floor in a dead faint. She recovered after a few minutes, and gulped down a brandy and soda brought by her husband, but immediately afterwards burst into a fit of weeping.

"His poor baby," she moaned, wringing her hands. "That's why she was so crazy to make you let them get married. Now they can't. What are we going to do . . . the shame of it."

In the way of hysterical wives she turned on her husband. "It's all you," she stormed. "If you hadn't told Johnny you wouldn't have him in the house as a son-in-law he'd be alive to marry her now." She went off in another flurry of tears.

"And if you hadn't agreed . . . " Worth began. "Oh, what's the use. The point is what to do with her."

4

THE inquest on de Frees was held in the church hall at Taceham, four days later. The county coroner sat with a jury of nine villagers, and a full gathering of the village attended to hear the evidence; there hadn't been an inquest held in Taceham within living memory. The Worths had returned to London after the discovery of the body, but had been warned to attend the inquest.

The first witness, Jonathan Hancock, described how he had been ploughing. "I'd started at the Downs side of the field," he said, "and I was on a run about ten yards from the Hall grounds when I feels me tractor give a kin'a jump, as you might say. Next thing I sees is a body." He described how he ran to the hotel and Commander Bowman telephoned the police.

Inspector Ross deposed that he saw the body on the ground beside a depression in the soil. He took measurements of the depth of the depression, and from those estimated that the body had been buried a foot deep.

Sensational evidence was given by Dr. Thomas Gimlett, the Divisional Police Surgeon. He said that he had conducted a *post mortem* on the body. The man was aged about thirty-five and was in a good state of health. He estimated that death had occurred between eleven and fourteen days earlier, probably twelve days. He found that the skull of the man had been fractured by a blow from some weapon . . .

"Can you suggest, Doctor, the nature of the weapon?" the coroner asked.

"Problematical, sir. It could have been caused by the spherical head of a poker, by a life preserver or the butt end of a revolver."

"But it killed him, Doctor?"

Doctor Gimlett havered for a few moments. "I would say it was not the entire cause of death, sir," he replied, "but it led to death."

"What exactly do you mean by that, Doctor? I thought a fractured skull would of itself prove fatal."

"Fracture of the skull even if extensive may yet be unaccompanied by injury to the brain, Mr. Coroner," the doctor said. "In this case there was no laceration of the brain which was, in fact, uninjured."

The coroner ruffled a hand through his scanty hair and eyed the doctor with a puzzled glance. "I don't quite understand," he complained. "The man had a fractured skull and you intimate that the brain was unaffected. Yet the man died."

"Well, sir, when I opened the body I found particles of soil and one or two grains of barley in the mouth and throat. This raised a somewhat serious conundrum. With Inspector Ross I went up to the barley field and from the spot where the inspector pointed out as that from which the body was unearthed, I took several samples of soil.

"At the County laboratory I examined through a comparison microscope the samples taken from the field and those exhibits I had removed from the mouth and throat of the deceased." He paused, dramatically. *"They corresponded in every degree."*

The room was now very still as the jury and the audience followed the doctor's evidence. The coroner fiddled nervously with the pencil with which he had been recording the evidence. Two reporters from local newspapers suddenly became alert.

"What do you assume from that, Doctor?" the coroner asked.

"The only way in which the particles of soil and grains of barley could have been drawn through the mouth and into the throat, sir, is by breathing. That is what I meant when I said that the fracture of the skull was not the entire cause of death, but led up to it. *The deceased was suffocated . . . "*

"You mean he had been buried alive?"

Gasps of horror ran round the room; the reporters scribbled madly in their notebooks after having dawdled through the earlier evidence.

"I mean that he had been buried before he was dead, sir."

"The same thing, surely, Doctor?"

"Not quite, Mr. Coroner. Let us not be dogmatic about it, and put forward an assumption. The man had been hit over the head with some weapon. In the darkness of night and without any lights, seeing him unconscious on the ground, they might have believed him dead — a reasonable assumption since he had been hit hard enough to fracture the skull. Left with, as they thought, a dead body on their hands, which they *had* to get rid of, they buried him, without the *intention* of burying him alive."

"I see. Had he not been buried and

thereby suffocated . . . "

"He would not have died, sir. The fracture was not sufficiently serious necessarily to cause death."

Mr. Norman Worth deposed that he lived in London but paid frequent visits to the Saxon Hall hotel. He was interested in the financial market. The deceased had been the guest of his wife and himself at Saxon Hall, staying for lunch and dinner. He left the same night . . .

"That would be the night of his death?" the coroner suggested.

"That I couldn't say, sir, but taking Dr. Gimlett's evidence of the time of death, it might well have been."

"You knew the dead man well?"

"No, sir. I had met him that day for the first time. He really came to spend the day with my daughter. They had an understanding."

"What time did he leave?"

"About ten o'clock. My daughter and I accompanied him to the Hall entrance, but we did not go outside;

there was a violent storm in progress. I saw him turn in the direction of the hotel car park and then I shut the Hall door. A few moments later I heard a car start up and go down the drive. I presumed it to be Mr. de Frees."

Miss Mary Worth, who appeared in a state of distress, was comforted by the coroner. "We will not keep you many moments, my dear young lady," he said. "You were engaged to Mr. de Frees and he came down to see you?"

"Yes, sir. And he was to telephone me from London the following day, but I heard nothing from that day until his body was found."

Inspector Ross rose. "Do you know, Miss Worth, what make of car Mr. de Frees drove?"

"Yes, sir. He owned a six-seater Austin Princess."

"What is the point, Inspector?" the coroner asked.

"On the morning following the deceased's visit to Saxon Hall, sir, a large Oldsmobile car was found in the hotel car park and could not be accounted for. It remained there for several days until we removed it at Commander Bowman's request. We still have it."

"I don't see . . . "

"The car has faked registration plates unknown to any registration authority."

"Have you reason to believe that the car has any connection with this tragedy?"

"Only by reason of the fact, sir, that there is no trace of the Austin Princess car which Miss Worth says Mr. de Frees always drove. It is not in his garage, and the caretaker of the flats says it has not been seen since it was driven away by de Frees on the day of his visit here."

The foreman of the jury rose. "Are you suggesting, Inspector, that Mr. de Frees drove the Oldsmobile car here — and that since the car was left, he never left the hotel on that night?"

"I have no firm reason for suggesting any such thing."

The coroner summed up. "This is a most inexplicable case," he said. "The deceased was seen by his host to leave the hotel and go towards his car in the hotel parking place. A car was heard to drive away. From that moment he disappeared from human ken until his body was found in a field in which he had been buried whilst still breathing. Except for the burying he would not have died had he received medical attention for the blow on the head. *It may occur to you that had he had been left to receive attention, he could have named his attackers*."

The jury without retiring returned a verdict of murder by some person or persons unknown.

De Frees was buried next day for the second, and last, time. There were no mourners at the graveside.

The last word was had by the Saxon Hall porter Jones, to the secretary: "I told you, Hall, that that there apparition as Miss Worth saw was a warnin'," he reminded her. "He allus appears afore an 'orrible death."

"Pshaw!" Miss Hall sniffed.

5

MURDER!

Inspector Ross cursed silently. There had been no murder in that part of the county since he had been elevated to his present rank; he, in fact, had never been engaged in a murder investigation, except as a uniformed constable, years before, assigned to make routine inquiries. Now, here he was head over heels in one — and one which he was expected to solve.

Chief Superintendent Wilton was equally pessimistic — for a variety of reasons. "Very awkward ... very awkward, indeed," he said. "Commander Bowman is a close personal friend ... inquiring into crime in his hotel ... lamentable. What are you going to do about it? Have to be careful ... influential man ... very old family."

"That don't concern me, sir. If he had anything to do with it, he's just the same as anybody else."

"Anything to do with it!" The Chief Superintendent nearly collapsed. "What the devil would he have to do with it, man?"

"It's his hotel and his barley field and the man had been staying there. He'll have to be investigated same as everybody else who was in the hotel."

The Chief Superintendent gave it up. "This Socialism and Jack's as good as his master is going to ruin the country," he said to himself. "It's anarchy. Now, in my young days . . . " He came back to facts, and went over the evidence. "He comes down to see the girl, spends a day with her and the family and goes off during a storm because he's an early appointment next morning. And London only about two and a half hours away. He *did* leave, I suppose?"

"The Worths saw him off the premises, sir."

"Then how comes it he's found buried in the ground he was supposed to have left? Did he come back again?"

The inspector pondered the question as he went over the hotel, mentally. "You mean to have spent the night *sub rosa* with the girl. It's a fact that she went right off to bed after he left."

"Could he have done?"

"Well, sir, her room is at the back of the hotel overlooking the parking spot. An iron fire escape runs up the building at the back, access to which could be gained, in case of fire, via her bedroom window." He shook his head. "I should say the idea is nonsense."

"Let's consider it, anyway. Suppose father had refused to agree to an engagement — he was against it, you said — and made it clear to de Frees during their talk. The girl gets the fact out of de Frees when he goes up the fire escape and into her room. He says your father says we aren't going to marry with his consent and money, so that's that. It's all off. She knows she's in the family way by de Frees, and now he's going to walk out on her."

"What did she do, sir? Hit him over the head with a poker — which there isn't a firegrate in the room — carry him down the fire escape and up to the barley field and bury him?"

"H'm! Quite so . . . Let's hold on to the one fact we know — that he was killed somewhere in the circumference of Saxon Hall. Nobody's going to kill him, say in London, and then cart the body all down here to bury it in a barley field, are they?"

"I'm not so sure of that, sir, about being killed at the Hall."

"Why not?"

"There's a matter of a car. The one left in the hotel car park which you know about . . . "

"The one in which he drove down for the visit. It's clear now why it was never claimed. De Frees was dead."

"No, sir. De Frees was a smart man expensively dressed. Can you see him driving a car like the one we have in our yard? And him expecting to marry a rich man's daughter. I reckon it could have been this way, sir. He was knocked off after leaving Saxon Hall, perhaps on the road, brought back here — you haven't to drive up to the Hall to get to the barley field, where he was buried as we found him. He was probably carried in that car, in the hollowed out seats."

"And what do you suggest happened to de Frees's own car, Inspector?"

"Those who killed him drove down in the old car and drove back in de Frees's Austin Princess, after shoving their old car into the hotel park."

"And how do you reckon the men knew about the barley field? Dammit, man, the field isn't next to a road. You can't drive past, see it, and say here's a good place in which to bury the body. Only people from hereabouts would know how to get to it."

"We haven't any murder thugs in these parts, sir."

"No? . . . There are thugs in every

part of the country, Inspector, but you don't know about them until they commit a piece of thuggery. You find those thugs. They're local, otherwise the body wouldn't have been buried where it was."

"Why should anyone want to kill the man here? He wasn't known in the place. I gather it was the first time he'd ever been down here, or visited Saxon Hall."

"Maybe it was Saxon Hall that was responsible. Let's make an assumption: de Frees says good night to Worth, starts up his car and drives to the gates and out on the road. Some of our locals see him leaving, may have heard him say good night at the door. People staying at Saxon Hall are pretty well heeled — all the local people know that. Right. De Frees is either signalled down or is followed by another car. It gets in front, is pulled across the road. The occupants get out, demand money from de Frees. There is a fight and de Frees gets hit over the head. They think he's dead, and they know where and how to get rid of the body. As locals they know how to reach the field from the road. They get him up there and bury him, thinking it pretty safe. They weren't to know that a damned great tractor was going to turn up the field within days, and find the body."

"They're out on spec, sir; but were provided with spades?" Ross said, sarcastically.

The Chief snorted. "You're a one for putting up a negative argument. They had all night to go fetch a spade, hadn't they? Was there any money found on the body?"

"No, sir."

"No wallet or purse?"

"No, sir. We'd have had a job to identify the corpse had not Miss Worth screamed out 'It's Johnny'."

"Well, there you are then. The fellow wouldn't be travelling over the country and staying in expensive hotels without any money. Robbery was the object. You take my word for it. And he was killed in the struggle for it."

The inspector was unconvinced. "How would anyone know he was leaving the Hall, sir? At that time of night — ten o'clock and in a blazing storm. How would they know he had ever come at all?"

Back in his office Inspector Ross called his sergeant and began to plan the course of the investigation. He was not much taken with his Chief's idea that local thugs were the attackers; he knew the local people from contact and contacts — and the Chief didn't. Full area inquiries had been made before the inquest. He decided that his first task was to get all that could be found about de Frees. The man was unknown in Taceham; he lived in London; and in the Metropolis, Ross decided, was where such information might be obtained. He rang up Whitehall.

"Scotland Yard — Records," a voice answered. "Who speaks?"

"Detective-Inspector Ross, West Sussex C.I.D. I'm on a murder investigation. Have you any information on an individual named de Frees, known as Johnny?"

"Any address?"

"Yes, Cheshire Court, Chelsea, in a flat there."

"We'll ring you back."

The reply came back within an hour. Inquiries had disclosed, it said, that de Frees did have a flat there which he had occupied for two years; but he was away at the moment. The caretaker did not know his whereabouts, but there had been inquiries for him by a Miss Worth, said to be his fiancée. They had nothing in Records against any de Frees.

Ross replied that he wanted assistance from the Yard, but not in the way of an investigating officer. Information about the habits and associates of de Frees would be welcomed. He added that he wanted examination by the laboratory of certain articles, including specimens of dust Hoovered from the deceased's clothes, the contents of his pockets and his fingerprints. The exhibits were being taken to the Yard by a detective constable.

"Will do," the voice said.

Worthing is fifty-eight miles distant from London. The detective constable made it by train. Six hours later he returned — in a Yard Squad car, driven by a sergeant-driver. The car contained beside the driver and the Sussex constable a man in plain clothes who walked into Inspector Ross's office.

The inspector glanced up at the entrance. "Inspector Ross?" the visitor asked: and received an affirming nod. "What can I do for you?"

"Detective-Inspector Robbins of Scotland Yard, and you can do quite a bit for me."

"Spill it, Inspector;" Ross sat down to listen.

"You made inquiries of Records about a man named de Frees?"

"I did, yes, and your people replied . . . " He sought out the written report of the recorded telephone conversation.

"That we confirmed the address and said that the man was away from home — yes, I know."

"Then, what . . . ?" Ross began, but a wave of a hand by Robbins silenced him.

"You sent by a constable matter for laboratory examination, including fingerprints?"

"That's correct."

"Good! You did us a favour. We've been looking for the owner of those dabs for a long time. We have in records three examples of them — one left on a lintel plate of a bank's door which was broken into. Another on a small piece of jewellery that was dropped by thieves after a raid; and a third left after a smash-and-grab."

"But you told me Records had nothing on a de Frees."

"Neither we had — until now. We had those three prints without a name. They were filed in the Latent Prints section. You've given them a name. Now, lead me to him, laddie."

Ross threw back his head and roared with laughter. "Are you any good at digging, Robbins?" he asked.

"Digging? What the hell . . . "

"Digging — unless there are sets of duplicate prints."

"Which there aren't — as you know very well. We've a million prints at the Yard and no two have ever been found identical in sixteen points of comparison. So let's have a dekko at this Mr. de Frees."

Ross laughed again. "That's where the digging comes into it. De Frees is six feet underground. He's buried."

"Damn and blast . . . How come?"

The tale was told again. "So we rolled the prints off the dead man's hands — precaution, you know, for record — and sent them to you at the Yard. 'Love's labour lost', to quote Shakespeare."

"Bacon," Inspector Robbins corrected. "But it isn't necessarily wasted. We know now that de Frees was a crook. We'll put out a hunt for his friends and acquaintances. Ever read Marcus Tullius Cicero, Ross? He wrote *pares vetere proverbio cum paribus facillime* — "

"Birds of a feather flock together," murmured Ross.

"Quite so. And he's been proved right throughout nearly two thousand years. I'll find out what species this de Frees mixed with in London. Mebbe, it will lead to your murderer."

"My chief thinks it's a local how-de-do."

"With a London crook in it. Why?"

"Come on a little trip and I'll show you."

They drove from the police station to Saxon Hall. Leaving the car in the hotel car park, Ross led the way up the slope, along the length of the herbaceous border and through the ornamental gates into the barley field. He paused at a disturbed spot of ground. "This is where we found your crook," he said. "Now, look around."

They were on a height of the South Downs. Beyond the barley field, itself built on a slope, the ground descended through and round other similar fields. Down below at the bottom of the slope ran a white ribbon of a road. "That's the road you came along," Ross pointed out. "All you can see of this from the road is just fields rising to this height. My chief's point is that no stranger would know this field existed, wouldn't know how to get here in the dark, so he says it's a local crime."

"And you don't agree. Why not?"

"Two reasons; and they're why I sent you the fingerprints and the other things. The fellow never visited these parts before that we know of. So why should anyone here, who didn't know him, bump him off? Secondly, on the morning after he was supposed to have returned to London, an old car with a hotted-up engine and hidey-holes under the seats was left in the hotel car park and remained there until

Bowman — he's the hotel proprietor — said he wanted it removed and we towed it away."

"How about the owner?"

"Don't know him . . . faked plates. No such registration."

"Then it looks as though you were right, and it isn't a local. Let's have a look at the car."

They drove back to the police station and into the garage. The car had been pushed to the back wall. Robbins walked all round it, held up the bonnet and peered into the works. "Nice hotting job," he said. "Done in a yard down in Limehouse by a chappie called Jack the Mek. Mek means mechanic," he explained.

"You know it?" Ross asked.

"Not from the Assistant Commissioner's Rolls Royce, laddie, but I know the Mek's work, though we'd never trace this one to him. We've never fixed anything on him yet. But we know."

"What is he?"

"Motor provider to the Underworld, London and the provinces. Claims he's as honest as the day is long. Tells our men when taxed, 'You know I'm always ready to help you boys whenever I can'. He's done so on several occasions by telling us where a wanted car could be found, and collecting a reward for doing so. Usually, the fellow with the car is one who has done Jack in the eye with the purchase money, and he's given him away. No, nobody gives him away to the dicks. Too useful."

"But doesn't the man *give* him away?"

Robbins laughed. "Not ruddy likely, he doesn't. The gangs would rub him out pronto. They depend on Jack the Mek for their cars. Give him a pinched car and in half a day he'll have so altered it that not even the owner can recognise it. New engine number stamped on, new chassis number, new number plate and a new logbook you couldn't tell from genuine."

"Then this is a London crook car?"

"Don't know about London. But it's a get-away car. Shove in some ethyl petrol and the only cars that could catch it are those which run round Montreux or Monte Carlo rally." He knitted his brows. "Wonder why the hell they abandoned it?"

"Better exchange value, Inspector," Ross suggested. "There's no trace of the car in which de Frees drove down here — an Austin Princess."

"So? I'll lay a pound to a bad penny it don't look like an Austin Princess now, not with a new bonnet and new colouring. It probably looks more like a Rolls. The Princess has a Rolls engine, anyway."

They went together to Saxon Hall for a meal. Commander Bowman was treated to the revealed facts.

"Oh, no," he wailed. "Not a friend of the Worths. I don't believe that. They aren't that sort."

"They're not likely to know anything about it, Commander," Ross said. "Faire feathers make faire fowles

69

according to Mr. Bunyan in *Pilgrim's Progress*, and money has no smell. De Frees had money, or so he said."

"Well, I'll be getting back to the Yard and set things going." Robbins started out towards the car. "Thanks for the hospitality, Ross I'll keep in touch with you in anything we unearth."

6

THERE were others than Miss Mary Worth who had been inquiring into the prolonged absence of Johnny de Frees: and were equally anxious to find him. Six men had been debating into the why and wherefore of it, whilst sitting round a table loaded with bottles and glasses in a fourth-floor room of a house in Magdalen Road, Wandsworth, which is within sight of the prison, in the interior of which two of the six had more than a passing acquaintance.

They were a disconsolate sextet in spite of the ample refreshment. Four days had passed since de Frees should have met them, one by one, in widely scattered parts, and to each handed old, soiled notes to the value of £1,400. He, as well as the money, which was more important at the moment, was

71

conspicuous by absence.

"Over ten thousand nicker," 'Red Mick' reminded the other five. (Red because of the colour of his hair and Mick because some long time back he numbered an Irish ancestry). "As sound a job as ever we done — and not a stiver for it."

The police at St. Albans were also anxious to get hold of the £10,000, which had been lifted from the International firm of Durand and Company, and was meant to go, instead, to their employees as wages for a week; but which had been hijacked on the way from the bank to the firm's premises.

"Ten thou," Red Mick said again. "He's gorn orf wid it, and we gets damn all."

"No. Johnny would'nae do that on us." This from Eddie Larkin, the six's strong-arm man who carried a gun. "Not Johnny. We're too valuable a team for him. Look, we've had twice ten thousand quid over the years and we'll get ten thousand again. Johnny don't kill the geese as collects his eggs for him."

"Then where the hell is he? An' why don't he phone? It's him as has the money stashed away — until the hunt had died down, he said."

It wasn't until five days later that 'Smiler' Jacobs called a meeting in the Wandsworth room, made the bold announcement, "Johnny's dead" and produced a Sussex newspaper with the report of the inquest in Taceham.

Sorrow was drowned by the inquiry, "Where's the lolly, then?"

"We don't know where he hung out," mourned the third of the six. They didn't; or they hadn't until now; de Frees kept his home a secret. The six's meetings, always held in the Wandsworth room, were arranged by telephone, and Johnny turned up there.

"I know where he cached," announced Smiler. He pointed to the newspaper. "Read it in there — Cheshire Court,

Chelsea. Now — ” They went into a huddle.

That night the caretaker of Cheshire Court answered a ring at the door of his basement flat. As he opened up and stepped forward because he couldn't see anybody, a hand clapped round his mouth, and another slapped him on the back of the neck. He was bundled inside and bound and gagged.

The two assailants, 'Red Mick' and 'Peter' Schneider (the 'peter' represented not a Christian name, but a calling. Peter in Underworld jargon is a safe, and Schneider was an expert opener of other people's safes) went upstairs to the flat and forced the door. De Frees's safe was clamped to a wall in his dressing-room, next to the bedroom, to guard against night surprises. Of chilled steel with a combination lock, it took 'Peter' half an hour to crack it, and then he pulled the door open.

The safe was completely empty — except for a card on the shelf.

It bore across the centre the laconic word 'THANKS', with underneath a red circle with a black line obliquely across it, and through it.

They carried the news back to Wandsworth. Two hours later the six men set out for the West End. They were armed with coshes, life-preservers and knuckle-dusters.

The trussed caretaker was found by a Missus Mop when she turned up at 8 a.m. to start her daily drudgery. Police questioning the occupants of flats arrived eventually at the flat of de Frees. Let in by the caretaker with his master-key, they saw the open safe. The card, left there by the earlier visitors, was taken to Scotland Yard. It was free of fingerprints, but it did not need prints for the C.I.D. officers to know the source.

"*Alii sementem faciunt, aliimetentem,*" said Ross jocularly. (He liked to air his scholarship). It meant, to construe it literally, 'some do the sowing, others the mowing.' His sergeant would have rendered it as 'diamond cut diamond'. For the red circle with the black stroke was the insignia of the second of the gangs preying on London. And the Yard, though they knew all about the gang operations had not as yet been able to point a finger either at the operatives, or the boss.

★ ★ ★

The day following the publication of the inquest proceedings on de Frees a telephone rang in a room in Notting Hill. "Yes?" answered a voice; and its owner recoiled at the blast which followed the recognition. "You double-damned fool, why did you leave the car in the hotel car park?" The voice, though furiously angry, yet had an air of culture.

"Boss, I . . . "

"You've put me and the others on the spot. Where's the Princess? At Mek's?" The phone went dead.

Twenty-four hours later a body taken

from the Grand Canal at Limehouse was identified as that of Daniel Timmins, a man with a record of robbery and violence. There were no injuries on the body. A verdict of accidental death by drowning was recorded by a coroner after an acquaintance had said that Timmins was drinking heavily the previous night and had staggered down the street.

It was long after that the police connected Timmins with the car left in Saxon Hall park; and by then the 'Boss's' remarks over the telephone, had become prophetic.

7

SIR EDWARD ALLEN, the Assistant Commissioner in charge of crime sat back in his chair in Scotland Yard, fitted his monocle into his perfectly good left eye, and stared through it at his visitor. Detective Chief Inspector Robbins had just ended a verbal report on his visit to Taceham.

The A.C. grinned a little. "So you didn't get your man," he said. "Somebody got ahead of you." He returned to seriousness. "Well, he won't be worrying us any more. That's one good thing to come out of it. We know, now, that he was involved in a jewel robbery, a bank raid and a smash-and-grab; his dabs have proved that. But what kind of a crook was he, Robbins? Drove an Austin Princess, had a luxury flat in Chelsea, in, apparently with tycoons of the financial world. I know Worth — got good connections. Any ideas?"

"Only problematical ones, sir. Take that flat. Luxurious is the word for it. And there was a pretty expensive Chubbs safe next to the bedroom . . . "

"I'm with you. Go on."

"Well, sir, we've handled a few raiders in our time, and searched their rooms, but never found a Chubb safe, and we've never found anyone flush with money after a raid. But when they've finished their sentence and been released from prison they've always had money to burn."

"You mean . . . ?"

"As I view it, de Frees was custodian of the loot until it was safe to circulate it, or dispose of the jewellery."

"And who would be trusted with the loot, Robbins?"

Robbins grinned. "I should say the planner, the architect of the raid, the organiser. In short . . . "

"The gang boss?"

"Quite so, sir."

"And you put de Frees in the role?"

The inspector produced the card taken from the safe. "'Thanks', sir and not a solitary stiver inside, not even papers. I reckon there had been a haul and a rival crowd knew all about it. I would say they knew de Frees was dead, guessed the doings would be in the safe, raided his place and abstracted the proceeds."

"That would mean that they knew about the murder."

"That's so. Yet there had been nothing in the papers until after the inquest proceedings. They wouldn't have got to hear of it by chance in London."

"Has there been a raid lately?"

"A hi-jacking of £10,000 at St. Albans, sir — a wages snatch, and no trace of the raiders or of the money. Usual procedure — delivery van pulled up in front of the firm's gates, crew handling a large case, apparently for delivery. Wages car appears, can't pass the delivery van. Men drop the case, approach the van with an apology for the delay, coshes come out. All over in a minute. Van drives off leaving the case in the middle of the gate. Found abandoned three hundred yards away, where getaway car was waiting."

"And you think that the proceeds vanished from the Chelsea safe?"

"It's reasonable, sir. There hasn't been any loot of note since."

"Well, now, Robbins, you promised information assistance to Sussex. What are you going to do about it?"

"Primarily, it's a murder inquiry, sir. I feel that Homicide could handle it better than myself."

Sir Edward stretched out a hand and pressed a button on his inter-com. "Manson," a voice came through.

"Allen, Doctor. I'm sending Detective-Inspector Robbins over to you. A homicide in Sussex with a London connection. They don't apparently want us, personally, but are seeking information about the London victim."

"Anything we can do, of course, Allen."

Robbins was ushered in on Commander Doctor Manson in his study adjoining the Yard laboratory. He saluted and stood by the elegant Sheraton desk which the Doctor had introduced from his pre-marital flat. "Sit down, Robbins," he greeted, "and have a cigarette." He passed over his own case. "This is our first meeting, I think?"

"Yes, Doctor. I'm on general duties, outside your *orbit*."

Doctor Manson settled himself in his chair. He is a doctor not of medicine, but of Science, and also a Barrister-at-Law, but did not practice; and also head of the forensic laboratory of the Yard which he founded while an amateur criminologist, and at the urgent request of the Assistant Commissioner. Six feet tall, he appears less by reason of a slight stoop from the shoulders the mark (nobody knows why!) of a scholar. His wide forehead is set above deep-set eyes which crinkle in the corners when he is absorbed in a problem. His fingers when his mind is deep in thought beat an annoying tapping on the arms of his chair — and when they are thus engaged, Yard men keep very silent.

The door opened and Chief Superintendent Jones and Chief Detective-Inspector Kenway entered, nodded to Robbins, pulled up chairs alongside Doctor Manson — and waited. They form with the Doctor what the Yard calls the Three Musketeers of Homicide: and to them go by order of the A.C. all cases of violent death for examination or inquiry.

"Now, Inspector," the Doctor said, "you apparently have a problem at second-hand. All I know from Sir Edward is that a man has been killed in Sussex, that he has London associations, and you have been asked, and agreed to make inquiries at this end. Since it is homicide you think we are the better able to help you."

"That is so, Commander." He

described the circumstances of the death and the result of his own inquiries into de Frees, including the discovery of the empty safe with its 'thanks' card. "There, sir, we are stuck," he said, "with the position *mortui non mordent*."

The Doctor smiled appreciatively; "*ne fronti crede*," he quipped back. "He is dead, but yet may speak. What do you know about him?"

"Only that he is — or was — a man about town, lived extravagantly and had plenty of money."

"From what source?"

"From nowhere we are aware of as yet, except . . . "

"Yes?"

"Something like £50,000 has passed into the hands of gangs during the last few months. We know that there are two gangs operating — our informers have told us that. We have suspicions of some of the operators, but the organisation is so good that we can't get any evidence against any of them.

I am pretty sure that de Frees is the head of one of the mobs."

"And he has been murdered and his gang robbed of their ill-earned loot?"

"By the other lot, sir. I think the card proved that."

Superintendent Jones giggled. They looked across at him. "We're . . . asked . . . find . . . murderer. Probably done . . . us . . . good turn," he said in his staccato jumps which the Yard called talking in shorthand.

"Come?" the Doctor invited.

"Easy . . . Raids planned . . . down . . . last details. Planner is . . . brains . . . the boss . . . gang carries out plan . . . just hoodlums . . . if boss dead . . . they're sunk . . . De Frees . . . boss . . . dead means his lot are scarpered . . . we don't get . . . more planned raids from them."

"I hadn't thought like that," Robbins said.

"Ah! Well, I got 'magination," Jones said.

It brought a howl of laughter from

Kenway. Jones's lack of any imagination was a legend in the Yard, equally with his legendary reputation for delving out hard facts.

"Let us get back to the known facts." The Doctor cut off the arguments and surmises. "You want information about de Frees. Now, who knew him? Where did he spend his time, and with whom? And how?"

"There's one who knows him all right — and very well, too," Jones said.

"Who?" Robbins asked.

"The Worth girl. She was engaged to him, wasn't she. I reckon she must know something about him. She was carted round by him, and must have met people he knew."

"What about her father and mother?" Kenway suggested.

"Worth didn't know him according to what he told Inspector Ross. Met him for the first time the day he visited the family at Saxon Hall. Engagement was not countenanced by him; in fact he opposed it. Called de Frees an Italian gigolo. I had a long talk with Ross about it," Robbins said.

"Then he's out. The girl seems the most likely source at the moment," Doctor Manson said. "Someone from here had better see her. And Jones — what about those canaries of yours who sometimes sing?"

"I'll feed 'em some bird seed, Doctor, pronto."

8

MR. WORTH stormed round the lounge of their Kensington home, pacing up and down on the carpet. He waved his hands and shouted at his wife sitting helplessly, her eyes red with spent weeping. He had reason for his display.

The family had been discussing the immediate future of Mary Worth. Something had to be done. Ellie Worth admitted. But what?

The family physician, called in, had confirmed the opinion — which they had not believed — given by Dr. Macrae of Taceham; there was no doubt, he said, that Miss Worth was several weeks gone with child.

Mrs. Worth had burst into tears anew. "We'll be shamed," she moaned. "All our friends. It will begin to show in a few weeks."

"Only thing is to get her away," Worth had said. "And as far away as possible, until after the child is born. Then get it adopted — if it is born alive. Ellie, you'd better go with her to Spain — I'll rent a villa and the birth can be there." He clapped a hand on a knee. "That's the idea. Then nobody will know. Afterwards she can come home, and we'll get her married. I'll see the Spanish tourist people tomorrow."

Mary had thrown an instant spanner into the works.

"*Not till the murderer of Johnny is found*," she said. "I don't move from here until he's arrested and sentenced."

It was then that Worth began his rampaging round the room. But his threats and her mother's pleading failed to move Mary from her stand. "If you won't do anything," she threatened, "I'll do something myself. I'll get an advance on my money and engage investigators."

"But, Mary," Mrs. Worth admonished, "it's the job of the police to find him. They're investigating. You know that nice Inspector Coleman who came to see you said they would do all they could, and he would let you know when they heard anything."

"That's right, my girl," Worth chimed in. "It's murder, and that means the police never give up, and they always get their man in murder. Scotland Yard will be called in. In the meantime you can be resting comfortably in the sunshine in Spain until the baby comes, and everything will be all right."

"When they've got him," Mary said again; and nothing would move her from that.

Worth left the house in a passion. In his club he confided his troubles to Oliver Hyams — and expected sympathy from him. Hyams was the man the Worths had hoped would marry Mary. He was a lawyer well-known in City circles and had the advantage in the eyes of the Worths of having long been in love with Mary — and still was. Why she had not responded to his love, in spite of her parents' ruses to leave the pair together, Worth could not understand.

Hyams listened in silence to Worth's tirade. He was puzzled — and might well be for the story had not included the fact that Mary was *enceinte*; it struck Worth that Hyams might still want the girl, but would probably think twice about it did he know that she was having a child by another man. No mention was made, either, of the proposed banishment to Spain: only the girl's determination to employ someone to seek her lover's murderer.

"But listen, Worth. Don't you want the fellow or fellows to be tracked down?" Hyams replied. "If Mary is determined to help the police, let her. I don't suppose the police will mind so long as they receive anything she may find out through her detective."

"I tell you, Hyams, de Frees was a wrong 'un. When Mary told her mother about him, I made inquiries in certain circles . . . "

"What circles? And have you passed on that to the police?"

"No. It was before all this happened."

"Nevertheless, they ought to know about it. You shouldn't withhold information from the police in a case of murder." He stopped suddenly and wrinkled his brows. "Especially since de Frees was killed practically whilst on a visit to you at Saxon Hall."

"What do you mean by that?" Worth said loudly.

"Nothing. Keep your voice down for goodness' sake. Members are looking at you. What I mean is that when the police get the fellow and find out that you knew something about him which you have not told them, they might regard you as having obstructed the police in their inquiries. And this is a case of murder, remember."

"It's only what I was *told*, Hyams."

"Then you should pass on the name of your informant to the police, in order that officers may be able to check on the facts. They might lead to the arrest, man."

"I'll think it over," Worth countered: collected his hat and left the club.

Hyams walked to his office in Chancery Lane in a state of mental perturbation. There was something about Worth that appeared foreign to his nature. The man though seemingly anxious to find the attacker of de Frees was yet keeping to himself information that might be of help to the authorities.

He had been some time in the office when, during a desultory reading of a Brief — desultory because Mary Worth was uppermost in his mind — an idea struck him with alarm. De Frees had been murdered by someone at present unknown to the police. But had de Frees known that he was in danger, and if so, from whom? The thought opened up grave possibilities. Had de Frees communicated his suspicions of danger to Mary Worth? He (Hyams) thought it unlikely in view of the girl's determination to hunt for herself, the killer; had she known anything she would certainly have told the police. Besides, she had been completely unsuspecting — as shown by collapse — on recognising de Frees's body on the stretcher at Saxon Hall.

But — and this was the thought which had alarmed Hyams — did the attacker or attackers know that de Frees had not told her of possible peril, and the source of it. Did they believe he might have done so, and that she would tell the police of his suspicions? If so, she was in dire peril herself. The assailants of the man would be obliged to take every precaution to safeguard themselves, and the removal of Mary might be taken as that kind of precaution.

The thought made him lose a heartbeat and put all thoughts of his Brief out of mind.

After deliberation he telephoned Mary, but found that she was out. Confiding to Ellie Worth his fears of the possible danger to Mary should she continue in her determination to start investigations through a private detective, he begged her to persuade her daughter to leave things to the police authorities.

Ellie Worth listened with fear in her heart, but with, she said, little hope that she could move Mary in her decision. She said so to Hyams. "Couldn't you see her yourself and impress on her how seriously she might be concerned," she begged. "I don't know how on earth she came to meet the man. Norman says he was a gigolo. Where she found him we don't know. You know we had pinned our hopes on you marrying her. So trustworthy and in a good position, Oliver."

"I had hopes that way myself," Hyams acknowledged. "All right, I'll try and see her one day."

Delays, as Shakespeare put into the mouth of Pucelle in sight of Rouen, have dangerous ends. Hyams from a sense of the shyness of a discarded lover, delayed. By then it was too late to avert a third tragedy.

Mary Worth, when Hyams telephoned, was out on what she had told her mother was a shopping expedition. But the only article she purchased was a twenty page cheap magazine filled with crime stories of a sensational nature. Over a cup of coffee and a sweet cake in a café, she scanned the pages devoted to advertisements: and half-way down a column came upon what she was seeking.

CONFIDENTIAL INQUIRIES made by a private detective (ex C.I.D.). Write or call, Danny Taylor, Apartment 0/12, Portobello Road, London W.2.

Twenty minutes later, she was confronting Danny Taylor over a cheap desk in a rather dingy office, the walls of which were decorated with photographs of groups of police officers holding prisoners, and a photograph of Taylor himself standing proudly alongside a uniformed chief superintendent of police.

"All my work," Taylor said, waving a hand in the direction of the reproductions. "Nearly fifty arrests of well-known criminals." He adjusted his tie, and fiddled with papers on his desk. "And what can I have the pleasure of doing for you, Miss . . . ?"

"Worth — Mary Worth." She related the story of de Frees and Saxon Hall: told it slowly, because Taylor was writing it down in a black-bound notebook. At the end, he leaned forward in satisfaction. "Right up my street, Miss," he said. "I investigated six cases of murder while I was in the Yard — that means Scotland Yard," he hastened to explain — "and we caught all the killers." He indicated three of the photographs on the walls, and acknowledged, benevolently, that other Yard officers had helped in the investigations.

"I want you, Mr. Taylor, to give your full time to this," Mary said:

thinking of the baby that would soon be betraying its presence. "I will pay you for that."

"Certainly, Miss Worth. Right now. I'll put off all other inquiries and concentrate" — a course that would not present many difficulties, since he had no other inquiries in hand; and hadn't had for many more weeks than he cared to recall.

"Now about payment?" Mary introduced the subject.

"Three pounds a day are my terms, Miss, with, of course, all reasonable expenses, such to be accounted for." The girl took a number of notes from a roll taken from her handbag. "Here is £50 in advance," she announced. She extracted a visiting card, "And here is my address and telephone number. But do not ring me before eight o'clock at night, and do not speak to anyone else."

Leaving the office, she walked down into Notting Hill Gate, where she hailed a passing taxicab and was driven home.

Mrs. Worth watched from a window, her paying off the cab and entering the house. "Had a good afternoon's shopping, dear?" she inquired.

"No, mother. They hadn't got exactly what I wanted." She made no mention of the detective or any arrangements she had made — much to the relief of Ellie Worth, who hoped that the arguments of her husband and herself had carried weight, and the girl's project had been abandoned.

Three days later, Oliver Hyams deliberating the suggestion of Mrs. Worth that he should speak to Mary in an endeavour to dissuade her from interfering with the work of the police, was still tormented by the problem of Hamlet: whether to let his love for her be his guide and by opposing her, end his hopes. She was that kind of a girl — resenting opposition.

Dropping in the Dilettantes Club for lunch, he spied Doctor Manson alone at a table — unusual solitude for him — and approached him. "May I join you?" he asked: and was answered by the scientist drawing up a chair. "Try the steak and kidney pudding," Manson advised. "Fattening, I know, but neither of us need heed that." Coffee and brandy followed the sweets, and was taken in the library usually deserted at that hour.

"If you can spare a few moments, Manson, I'd like your advice and help," Hyams said; and was invited to take his time over the problem. He began the story of Saxon Hall, and was halted by the doctor. "I know all the details of the murder, Hyams," he said. "But I don't see how you are affected. You didn't have any dealings with de Frees, did you?" He stopped suddenly. Into his mind came certain recollections and an acquaintance. "Is this something to do with the Worth daughter?" he asked.

Hyams nodded. "Frankly, I'm scared, Manson. She's very headstrong, and has always had her own way. Now, she's intent on hiring a private detective to find the murderer of de Frees. Her parents have talked to her, but they don't see what I see — that if the person or persons responsible for de Frees's murder think she is probing into them through a private detective, they may be more than anxious to end such inquiry."

"By ridding themselves of Mary, do you mean?"

"It is in my mind, yes. Not being a cop or a dick, or whatever you call them, a private eye might hear about things your men wouldn't be told in the underworld, and if he turns them over to the police and the news gets round that he's working for Mary, well . . ."

"It is a possibility, though a remote one," Manson said. "I should not think they will attract further attention on themselves by another murder. Still, I think it would be a good thing if you had a quiet talk with her and explained the possible danger. And — "

There was a momentary hesitation and an air of constraint about the scientist. "And — what, Manson?" Hyams asked. Doubt and indecision clouded the Commander's brows, and when at last he spoke it was softly and slowly. "I shouldn't tell you this," he said, "but it may help you. We know de Frees to have been a crook engaged in robbery and violence. He has, however, no convictions against him because — " The doctor explained the fingerprints to which the Yard could put no owner until after de Frees was dead. "I think, perhaps, I will go along with you as an officer of the law when you see Miss Worth, and we can impress upon her together the inadvisability of her getting mixed up in the affair."

9

THE Bowlers' Arms is a hostelry situated in the Kilburn Park Road, in London, N.W.6, just before it joins Carlton Vale and Cambridge Gardens. The house is of considerable antiquity in its main part, but has been almost rebuilt and enlarged, with a tea garden rivalling the gardens of the old Bell Tavern, that eighteenth-century refreshment house which adjoined the once famous Kilburn Wells, on what is now Belsize Road.

Before its rejuvenation, it was named the Navigation Inn: an apt cognomen of the time, for navigators were busy in the area. Navigators was the name given to labourers digging the canals, railways and roads of England. The name has been corrupted these days to 'navvies': except that the navvies of today prefer to be known as road operators. When the old inn was remodelled and renovated, it became a free house, and the new proprietors changed the name to the Bowlers' Arms, and transformed the trade from the old-time company of navvies and their like to a more cosmopolitan section gathered from its immediate proximity to Kilburn Recreation Ground, with its facilities for games, etc. These included the now popular Bowls.

It is a pleasant refreshment house with a saloon bar nicely furnished with tables and chairs, and divided from the public bar in which standing only is the custom. On Saturday nights an entertainment is provided by two or three artists, relics of the now vanished Music Hall; and by a sing-leader for choruses which wound up the evening. The customers were pretty regular in their attendance, being known mostly by their Christian names.

On the night following the discovery

of the empty safe and the 'thanks' card in the flat at Cheshire Court — which was a Saturday — five men proceeded by Underground to Belsize Park, and then went on foot towards the Kilburn Park road. They walked separately.

In the Bowlers' Arms drinks were flowing to the satisfaction of the manager and the customers, and entertainment under their influence was becoming a little exuberant. A woman artist whose appearance hardly echoed the words of her song, was belting out, 'Oh, you beautiful doll,' and was joined in the chorus by the combined choirs of the saloon and the public bar. In a corner of the room, a little coterie of men sat together, tankards in front of them. The tankards had been refilled a number of times, and a convivial spirit was being evinced by the group.

The five lone walkers joined up outside the tea gardens. One of them approached the saloon entrance, pushed slightly open the door and peered inside. He rejoined his companions.

"They're there," he announced.

Suddenly, the Beautiful Doll came to a violent end when the saloon door was thrown violently open at the same moment that the public bar door banged back. Five men stormed in, pushing aside drinkers in their path, and converged on the corner table. The group, catching sight of them rose to their feet. In the free fight that developed, havoc ensued. Chairs, used as weapons, were smashed, glasses broken and one, thrown at the back of the bar smashed a large mirror which ran behind and along the full length of the bar. Bottles, jugs and a welter of beer and glass fragments littered the floor.

Attempts to eject the contestants were received with knuckle-dusters and coshes. For three or four minutes pandemonium reigned throughout the house. A barman sneaking out of the private entrance dialled the police. With the sounds of a police car siren in the near distance, the intruders pushed a way through to the tea gardens entrance and disappeared.

Police officers of 'X' Division stared in astonishment at the scene which met their eyes. The saloon bar was a shambles, with pieces of chairs and tables mixed up with broken glass. The exhibition of drinks and tankards at the back of the bar had vanished. Customers were dabbing handkerchiefs on cut faces, or bathing bruises from knuckle-dusters.

"What the hell has been going on here?" a police sergeant demanded; and was told of the descent of the army of five men. "Know any of 'em?" he asked. A barrage of shaken heads answered the question.

Behind the remnants of the corner table, one of the company who had been drinking there was lying unconscious, apparently from a hard smash on the chin. "He's one of the lot who were fighting," the manager said. He was promptly hauled up, brought back to consciousness, and then bundled off to the police station, where he spent the night in a cell.

He appeared in court next morning under the name James Hanna, and pleaded not guilty to a charge of causing a breach of the peace, and another of doing damage, with others, to the amount of £200.

Superintendent Jones, who had been wandering round the purluis of Paddington, looking for something, and had called in at the Kilburn police station on his way back, caught a glimpse of him as he was escorted to the Black Maria on the way to the court.

"Stone the crows, if it ain't Boxin' Jim," he said.

"Know him, Super?" the station sergeant asked.

"Know 'im? 'Course I knows him. Regular customer time ago. Very violent cuss. Three convictions . . . ought't been more only we couldn't pin him down. What's he been nabbed for?"

They told him. "Stone the crows,"

he ejaculated. "Bust me. What the hell's he doing round here? He don't ever leave up West."

"Well he might'a gone West for good in the pub last night. Place looked as if a typhoon had blown through it."

Jones sat in court throughout the hearing. In his defence Boxing Jim explained the happenings of the evening before. "Me and the others," he said, "were sitting in a corner of that pub drinking and listening to a doll singing when the door opens and a bunch of hoodlums comes in and went for us with weapons. Your Worship, we had to defend ourselves, they looked as if they was goin' ter lay us out. When they starts breakin' up the furniture and throwing glasses, we reckoned as we'd better get out. Then I receives a wallop on the chin and when I comes to, I wuz in the hands of the coppers. Lumme, sir, we never started anything. We wuz attacked."

"Did you recognise any of your attackers?" asked the magistrate.

"No, sir. They wuz wearin' nylon stockings over their heads."

"Any reason why they should go for you, and nobody else in the house?"

"Nary a one, sir. We wuz all law-abiding citizens." A grim smile appeared on the face of the Chief Detective in charge of the case. He was, however, unable to say anything about his knowledge of the prisoner until the magistrate had found him guilty, and asked if anything was known about him.

The manager of the Bowlers' Arms agreed in his evidence that the intruders burst into the premises and made at once for the corner company of which the prisoner was one. No, he said, he didn't know any of the men in the corner; it was the first time, he thought, that they had visited the hotel.

The magistrate, after deliberating for some moments, said there were circumstances of which he had not been told. It was an extraordinary thing for men to break into the public house and make for a specific number of men without any apparent reason. It was, he supposed, a natural consequence that they should protect themselves. But why had the prisoner's associates not come forward to give their version of the affray? On the whole he did not think there was sufficient evidence of guilt, and the prisoner would therefore be discharged.

"Cor lumme," said Jones as he left the court and walked away, looking thoughtful.

Back in the Yard, Old Fat Man picked up a telephone and asked for an outside line. To the girl who answered the ring, he gave a number. It was a couple of minutes before an answering voice broke in with "Who the hell is it?"

"Walker there . . . ? What . . . ? Oh, a friend." A minute later another voice said, "Yus?"

"Snoopy," Jones said. "Talkie . . . Usual place, two o'clock."

Kenway, overhearing the cryptic conversation, looked up. "Who's Snoopy? Fancy name for one of your dolls?" he asked jocularly.

"One of me canaries," Jones said. The fat superintendent had a number of canaries, or noses, or narks, or snouts, according to which variety of Underworld slang you preferred. Snoopy Walker was the pick of the bunch, and had been purveying information to the superintendent for years.

"Ruddy wonder he ain't had his singin' cut off long ago," Jones volunteered. "He's shopped a packet in his time."

"How do you do it, Fat Man?" asked Kenway whose 'noses' had either been shopped themselves or had desisted in passing on information on being detected or suspected of narking.

"Cause nobody ever seen me talkin' to him," Jones said, "They ain't never seen me with him. That's how."

At 2.10 p.m. Jones waddled into a public house on the North Circular Road, and near Hendon Stadium.

He went into the public bar. Half a dozen drinkers were busy downing refreshment — including a little runt of a man in a coat and trousers too big for him with a muffler round his neck. His shifty eyes were wandering between the door and a half-pint mug nearly empty of beer. Jones took a casual stand by his side. This was Snoopy.

"Double whisky, landlord," Jones ordered. "And soda." The little runt looked at him and then at the dregs in his own mug. Jones saw the look. "And landlord, give this geezer a pint of wallop."

"Bless you. You're a gent," the runt said. Each took a swallow from their drink. Looking at the television set, which was showing a cricket match in progress, Jones spoke out of the corner of his mouth. It was an accomplishment acquired through years of practice — and it was perfect; nobody had ever seen his lips move or his mouth show any evidence that he was talking; and nobody had ever heard what he had to say except the intended listener; he beamed his voice.

"Some chaps lifted ten grand out'a snatch," he said to Snoopy.

"The Liverpool lot," Snoopy said, also out of the side of his mouth. He took a swig from his wallop. "They ain't got it now, guv."

"Red Circle nicked it."

"An' got beat up — last night."

"De Frees the banker, Snoopy?"

"Sure, guv."

"And he was outed. Who?"

"Red Circle — so I hears."

"Why?"

"Summat personal, so the talk goes."

"Personal? To whom?"

"The boss."

"Ah!" Jones nearly spoke aloud in his excitement. "The boss. Who is he?"

"Don' know, guv."

Jones ordered another whisky while he thought that one out. It looked as though Snoopy was out to put up the kitty. (He usually got a couple of pounds for information). "It's worth a fiver, Snoopy," he intimated.

Snoopy's face twitched a little in acknowledgement of the super's thoughts. "Ef you makes it a ton, I still don't know, guv," he said. (A ton in crook talk is a hundred pounds).

"We've tags on one of 'em — from last night."

"He can't tell yer, neither. None of 'em knows the boss."

"Come off it, Snoopy. They has to be organised and coached."

"S'trait, guv. They ain't never seen 'im. They gets a phone message, an' then a drawn up plan for a snatch or a raid reaches 'em, and they don't know 'ow it gets there, all typed and detailed. Blue print, they calls it."

But the doings, the spondulics: what about them? Who's got the ten grand they lifted from de Frees's lot? Where's it gone?"

"Ain't no idea of the banker."

Jones admitted defeat. "Well, Snoopy," he said, "keep your ears open and keep in touch." The side of the mouth conversation ceased and Jones spoke openly and friendly. "Give him another half," he said to the barman, paid for it, and went out. Snoopy waited to finish his extra drink, and followed. He felt in his left-hand jacket pocket, and extracted three pounds which had got there as if by magic.

Doctor Manson listened to the tale told by Snoopy to Superintendent Jones, and thought it over very carefully. "Is he trustworthy, Fat Man?" he demanded. "It sounds a very peculiar business."

"You can bank on what he says, Doctor. He's on the fringe of the Underworld, has been a thief and would sell his mother for a fiver if he wasn't scared of being caught, but he's never fed me a stumer, and we've had some damn good tips from him, as you well know."

"And nobody knows the boss-man of the Red Circle. What's your idea of that?"

He waited with some anxiety for the answer, for on it much depended.

116

Jones knew the Underworld as no other Yard officer had ever done. A host of the gang leaders, and rank and file, were known to him by name and countenance. He could on hearing details of a raid or a break-in give the name or names of the operators; and all that was required was for the Yard to get the necessary evidence. The *modus operandi* files of Records in the Yard were not so reliable as Jones's know-how.

Old Fat Man took time to frame his answer, delving with his knowledge into the ways of crooks. When he spoke his words came slowly and with confident deliberation. "I reckon, Doctor," he said, "that the fact that nobody, not even his own men, knows who he is, and ain't never seen him, at least not to their knowledge, means that the boss of the Red Circle ain't one of the Fraternity. It ain't possible, if he were, that some of the noses ain't tracked him down, either for their own satisfaction, or for the purpose of putting a little 'black' on him."

"You mean he's an outsider, organising crime to be carried out by a gang?"

"That's how I see it, Doctor."

"And doing well. On a commission or percentage?"

"You can say he's doin' well again! Five of the biggest coups over the past three years have been by his lot." Jones spread his hands in a gesture of admiration for perfection. "He's a ruddy genius, Doctor whoever he is. We ain't recovered a brass cent from the loot, and though we know damn-well who the operatives are, we ain't never been able to get a whisper of evidence against 'em. Working on percentage or commission? . . . Not ruddy likely. I reckon it's a share-out basis."

An hour later Inspector Ross in Taceham lifted his telephone receiver in answer to a ring. "Ross? . . . Robbins here from the Yard. You can put a flea in the ear of your chief constable, son. The de Frees job was a London do."

A chuckle greeted the announcement. "Good . . . Thanks, Robbins. I'll give it to him."

10

DANNY TAYLOR, recovering from the shock of being presented not only with a job of detection, but also with a packet of fifty pounds in good new banknotes, and the prospect of a hundred or two more before his task was completed, set out on the following night on an investigation safari, having first fortified himself with what Louisa Carroll Thomas rhythmically put:

How odd it is that a little Scotch
Can raise Dutch courage to highest
pitch.

He wandered from Portobello Road down to Oxford Circus and on into Soho. His years as a C.I.D. man had brought him a number of contacts among a certain class of men who played it close to the law. One of these was a character known as Scotch Jock, and the name did not refer to Scotland. Taylor had done the man a service and was owed several *quids pro quo* for it. After visiting several ports of call, sampling the brew in each of them, he ran across 'Scotch' in a strip-tease club of a very lurid nature, enticed him to a corner of the bar, and began to ply his trade.

"Got a job, Scotch," he announced, "and with lots of gelt coming, and some of it is goin' to stick to your dollies. You owe me something, you know."

"Bonzo! What's it all abaht?"

"Pushing off Johnny de Frees."

Scotch stared at him. "Who the hell cares about Johnny?" he asked.

"Dame named Worth . . . classy dame . . . rolling in it."

"What's it got to do with her?"

"She was going to marry him. Now she wants the bloke who outed him. Any ideas, Scotch?"

"Nary a one, Danny. And if I had I wouldn't spill it. With Johnny gone there's more pickings for us. I'd sooner put up a handsome memorial tablet for him."

"That won't land you in gelt, Scotch. Say twenty-five per cent of what I make out?"

"I'll go through the grafters and give you a tinkle. Where are you now?"

Taylor wandered off to a gaming club in Cheapside, to still another in Kennington and arrived back in the Portobello Road at three o'clock in the morning in a high state of intoxication. Before that, however, a telephone had rung at a certain number, and from it the voice of a recording instrument drawled: "Please leave your message." Scotch Jock spoke slowly and distinctly of the inquiry that had been made of him by Taylor, and then rang off.

At eight o'clock next evening after a day spent in fruitless inquiries Taylor rang the Worth residence. A maid, answering, went through to the lounge with the intimation: "A telephone call for you, Miss Mary." Mary received a long report from Taylor to the effect that he was making progress and expected to have good news within a day or two. She replaced the receiver with a feeling of pleasant satisfaction.

She was, however, less pleased by the visit of Doctor Manson and Oliver Hyams, a visit paid in response to Mrs Worth's plea to Hyams. They appeared after the dinner hour and were received with pleasure by Ellie Worth, but somewhat coldly by Worth himself.

"I don't want Mary or myself worried by further police inquiries," he said when the reason for the visit was made known. "We have given all the information we know. Really, this eternal questioning is amounting to persecution."

"You must remember, Mr. Worth, that a man has been murdered after a visit paid to you . . . " Doctor Manson began.

"And after he had left us."

" . . . And that your daughter was to have married him. We are hunting for the assailant."

"So am I," Mary broke in. "The police don't seem to be getting anywhere, so I've made my own arrangements for finding him."

"Mary, I told you to leave things alone and trust to the police," Worth broke in.

Hyams looked distressed. "Listen, Mary?" he said. "Don't do anything like what you told your mother. It is dangerous. You are a sensible girl and you must realise that there was some reason why Johnny was killed and hidden."

"I can tell you why he was killed, Miss Worth," Manson said. "It will probably distress you, but you ought to know. De Frees was known to us to be a man with a record of violence, was a gangster . . ."

"I don't believe it. You're telling me lies," Mary almost shouted. "I knew

124

Johnny, and he was as gentle as a lamb."

"If it will convince you, Miss Worth," Manson insisted, "I will let you see his record in the files of Scotland Yard."

"Mary," Hyams leaned forward. "It could be dangerous for you to interfere. Suppose the people who killed Johnny think he told you something they wanted to know from Johnny. You'd be in danger from them. Leave it to the police. They're used to handling things like this."

"I will add my plea to that," Manson said.

The girl grinned. "Too late, Oliver," she announced. "I've engaged a private detective. He telephoned me tonight saying he's making progress and expects to be able to give me a name in the next day or two."

"Oh, my God!" Worth exploded.

"Who is he, Miss Worth?" Doctor Manson waited for the answer.

She smiled. "Oh, I'm not telling the

police that. You'd only try to stop him. He was in the C.I.D. once, so he knows how to go about things."

They gave up the attempt.

"Tell me, Miss Worth — " the Doctor went off on a different tack — "how did you meet Mr. de Frees, and where?"

"In the Nite Lite Club."

"The Nite Lite! How on earth did you come to be in a place like that?"

"A schoolgirl friend who goes there told me it was an entertaining place, so I went to see."

"And Mr. de Frees was there?"

"Yes, he came in with two other men and they sat at a table together. When the two men left he came across, asked if I was a new member and could he share my table because he never liked being alone. After that we used to meet there regularly."

"You told him who you were?"

"Of course. He said he was a business man making a lot of money."

"He was never in business in his life,

Miss Worth," Manson said. "Don't ever go in the Nite Lite again. It has a dreadful reputation. And if you will take my advice you will drop that school friend who frequents it." Mr. Worth accompanied them to the door. "I'm glad you came, Hyams," he said. "And you, Doctor. How is the investigation going?"

"We are getting somewhere, Mr. Worth, slowly, but not, apparently, as fast as your daughter's private eye."

Back in the Yard, Doctor Manson sought out Superintendent Jones. "Can you name a former C.I.D. man who has turned to private detection, Fat Man?" he asked.

"You mean still alive, Doctor?" Manson nodded. "One has been engaged by the Worth girl to find de Frees's killer, and says he expects to have a name in a day or two."

"I know of one," Jones said after a mental search back in records. "A man named Taylor, Danny Taylor. He was a bent dick, and was caught out and chucked off the Force. Advertises in crime and detection story papers. Lives in the Portobello Road. If that's him, then the Worth girl will get rooked well and proper. Want me to pop in and see him?"

"Not at the moment, Fat Man. If he's bent, he probably has sources of information we can't call on. He may drop on to something and we can probably get it out of her. By the way, she met de Frees in the 'Nite Lite'."

"The Nite Lite!" Jones was staggered. "How the hell did a girl like her get in there? There ain't a ruddy member who ain't crooked."

★ ★ ★

A man entering a flatlet switched on the answering recorder attached to the telephone and started up conversations that had come over the wire. He betrayed only a passing interest until there came to his ears Scotch Jock's

128

message. Then he sat down and called six numbers. To each of the persons answering he gave the same message. There were six replies, equally laconic, to his call: "Right, boss."

11

SIR EDWARD ALLEN, Assistant Commissioner (Crime) presided over a conference called in his room at Scotland Yard at which, in addition to Doctor Manson and Superintendent Jones were the Chief Inspectors of 'A', 'C', 'D', and 'E' divisions which policed the thronged and cosmopolitan neighbourhood of Charing Cross, Piccadilly, Regent Street, Oxford Street, Soho and Tottenham Court Road.

Rumours of forthcoming trouble in the West End were filtering through to the divisions by way of 'grassers'. No finger was being put on the kind of trouble: just a feeling of excitement among the Fraternity that something was going to move.

Superintendent Jones entertained a suspicion; and it was never wise to ignore the glimmerings in Old Fat Man's mind when it began to work on things criminal. The A.C. always held that Jones was the original example of Extra-sensory Perception.

The superintendent aired his thoughts. "I think it's going to be retaliation for the killing of de Frees," he said. "Johnny was the boss man of a mob. He's gone, and I guess it's going to throw his manor into the other crowd, and Johnny's ain't goin' to surrender their territory without a fight. They've netted something like £50,000 from it over the past three or four years; they'll get damn all in the future if the others cash in on them."

The Chief Inspectors nodded *en masse*.

"Then we'd better look after their leader, Jones," the A.C. said. "Who is he?"

Jones chuckled, a grim chuckling. "We don't know," he said. "And they don't know, either. He's the voice that breathed o'er Eden, so to speak."

"Meaning by that, Jones?"

"That all they know of him, A.C., is a voice over a telephone which, so far as they are concerned, hasn't got a number. They can say with Thomas Hardy — your countrymen, A.C. since you're a Dorchester man — 'I heard a voice I know not where'."

"How do you know all this, Jones?"

"From me 'noses', A.C."

"But the gang can't work out raids from a voice — the mob, I mean."

"They don't. The man's a wizard. Every detail of the programme for a raid, to a time schedule, is typed out with six copies. A copy goes to each operator . . . "

"How?"

"It's deposited at an announced place — six different places — and picked up at a given date and time. And it includes all the alibis, and the nature of disguises where necessary."

"And nobody knows the author — the boss?" the A.C. asked.

"Nobody, A.C. My 'nose', Snoopy,

and he's the best in town, says all they know is that he's a toff, talks like one, and if anyone goes outside the script just once he's finished."

Jones sat back in his chair and wiped perspiration from his brow. A remarkable feature about his address, noted by Doctor Manson and the A.C., was that in his earnestness, Old Fat Man had forgotten his usual staccato, shorthand speaking; his words had flowed evenly and easily. Suddenly, as though remembering something he had meant to say, he leaned forwards again. "Every damned thing he has planned to date has come off." He looked round. "You all here know that, and we've never caught one of his men."

"And you think, Fat Man, that with de Frees dead this lot are going after the de Frees manor?" Doctor Manson asked.

"I think that's one idea, Doctor; but I've a sneaking idea that that wasn't the only reason for de Frees's death. I gotta idea there was something personal in it."

"By Jupiter, gang war!" The A.C. shot out the words in a shocked voice. "We haven't had a gang war for years. What can we do in the way of restricting operations?"

Jones said: "I was down in Kilburn the other day. Some men had wrecked a bar in a public house and attacked four men drinking in a corner — "

"Yes, I read about that in a report," the A.C. said. "One of the attacked men was knocked out, picked up by two of our men and charged with a breach of the peace. He pleaded not guilty and witnesses said he had nothing to do with the attack, but was a victim of it. The magistrate discharged him. That the case, Jones?"

"That's right, A.C. He was a character by name Dalby, known as Boxing Jim. Why do you suppose that he and the others were attacked in the pub?"

"You tell us, Fat Man," the A.C. invited.

"Because they had had their bread-winner taken from them and reckoned on who were the killers, or rather who was the killer."

"De Frees?" Manson asked.

"Yes, and because they lost £10,000 from Johnny's safe. Boxing Jim is a drummer from the Red Circle mob."

"Drummer?" the A.C. asked.

"Means a man who looks out for a likely place to screw, sir."

Jones explained.

"Screw?" The officers grinned. One of them explained: "A screw, sir, is a crook word for a break-in and robbery."

"Also," Jones came in again, "he's the strong-arm when there is trouble in the family. If you like to pull him in on a trumped-up charge, I'll have a go and see if I can extract something from him. I'd like to know what they were doing in Kilburn."

"Do you know the other three men, Jones?" Manson asked.

"No, I never saw them. I wasn't down there until next day. The three scarpered when the police siren was heard."

"Wouldn't it be better to circulate the offer of a good reward among informers asking for anything they can find out?" an inspector asked.

"Lor love a duck!" Jones burst out. "The grassers wouldn't touch it if you offered a 'grand'. Not with that mob. They'd never live to spend it, not with the grapevine working."

A couple of constables picked up Dalby in Piccadilly Circus and carted him off to the West End station on a charge of loitering with suspicious intent. Jones waddled his eighteen stone down there. He put on his best baby-face smile and sympathetic voice when he was confronted with Dalby — and when he tried those two achievements, Old Fat Man could nearly charm blood out of a stone.

"Well, well, Jim, son, you seem to be landing in a mort o' trouble these days," he began. "Knocked out in a pub by some of the other mob, and now loiterin' in the Circus . . . "

"I wasn't loitering, Super. I was waiting for a pal what had gone in the Gents."

"Had a bit of a walk, didn't he, Jim? There ain't one anywhere near where you wuz. You want to be more careful, Jim. The boss won't like you keeping on gettin' in the hands of the busies just when he's plannin' somethin'. You'll be gettin' a telephone call, son."

Jones noted that Dalby had started slightly at the statement that the boss was planning something, and he elaborated. "With Johnny out'a the way, youse reckoning on his manor, so the grapevine says."

"You kidding me, Super? I ain't got no boss and I ain't planning nothing. You're thinking of somebody else."

"Then why did your lot bump off Johnny?"

"Our lot? Who's our lot?"

Jones shrugged his shoulders. "All right, Jim. You'll probably get six

137

months for this, with your record, and that'll be too late to join in the doings, and the boss won't want a newly convicted bloke. A conviction goes down in *modus operandi*. Now if you knew anythin', just a teeny-weeny whisper which wouldn't get out of this 'ere cell, then we'd settle for seven days. See?"

It didn't work. Fat Man never had any hope that it would; but he had to try it.

"Go to hell," Dalby said. "I won't get even seven hours. I'll call me pal to say why I was waiting for him, and where we were going when he come out."

Jones grinned at him. "Oh no, you won't, Jim boy. If you did there'd be a new member of the Red Circle."

At the court that morning, Dalby was placed on probation. After hearing a solicitor on his behalf, the magistrate said there seemed to be a genuine doubt, in spite of the defendant's record.

12

OVER the space of a week five calls went for Mary Worth to the house in Kensington. Mr. Taylor sounded quietly confident that he was getting a clue to Johnny's killer. He had, he told her, contacted a man who had promised to scout round in certain circles he knew of, and would be ringing him with news very soon. Scotch Jock was his *alter ego*.

Then, for four days she heard nothing from or of him. On two visits she paid to the Portobello Road she found the office closed and locked; and her telephone calls subsequently were unanswered. Then, at eight o'clock on the fifth day a ring came. The maid, summoning Mary, said, "The gentleman says please be quick. It's very urgent." Mary hurried to the instrument. "Mary Worth," she announced.

"Taylor," said the caller, and sounded very agitated. "For God's sake, Miss, pack in this investigation. It's dangerous. I'm quitting and returning your money. There's a man — "

"But Mr. Taylor, I'm . . . " What she was going to say was never sent across. There came over the wire the sound of a scuffle and then a bang as though the telephone receiver had been dropped and banged against a wall or table leg. Mary jiggled her receiver until the exchange came on and asked had she not been connected. "I was cut off in the middle of a talk. Please try to reconnect me." A moment or two later, "I can't get any reply," the exchange said.

That evening Mr. and Mrs. Worth came to a decision and announced the fact to their daughter the following morning over breakfast. "I'm fixing up a furnished flat in Benidorm, Spain, today, and you and your mother leave by air on Saturday, on a plane to Valencia. And a nice figure the damned flat is costing me, I can tell you."

"I'm not going until — " Mary began.

"You're going on Saturday. Look, you stupid little bitch, in a week or two that brat you are having will begin to show itself. If you think I'm going to have our friends know you're having a bastard, you've a new think coming. As for de Frees, he was a damned crook and you should be ashamed of yourself for ever getting into his clutches — you and your money he wanted."

"He wasn't — "

"Don't be an even bigger damned fool, girl. The police have his record on paper."

Oliver Hyams, told by Worth of his daughter's condition, expressed sympathy with Mrs. Worth and supported the decision to send the girl away for the birth. "I'll make inquiries, Worth," he said, "and see if de Frees left any estate. If so, we will claim damages for seduction. What will you do about the child?"

"Have it adopted. I'm not having anyone find out that she's had an illegitimate child by a bloody crook. Sign the brat right away to anybody. I'll leave the matter in your hands as my lawyer."

The Saturday flight to Valencia failed to materialise. On the Friday morning — the day before the flight — a Mr. Stevenson stopped a constable patrolling his beat along the Portobello Road. "Constable," he said, "I'm a little worried over a tenant in number three of my house, a Mr. Taylor."

"What's he been up to, sir?"

"Nothing that I know of. It's like this. He apparently hasn't been in for days and his newspapers are spilling all over the floor outside. The telephone people complain that his number is persistently ringing, as though the receiver has been left off."

"That's funny, Mr. Stevenson. Do you think he might be ill, or something? I'll come along and have a look-see. Have you got a spare key? If so, bring

142

it along in case we have to go inside the flat."

They mounted the staircase to the second floor. Stevenson had not exaggerated; several newspapers lay scattered half-way under the door and half out in the hall. The constable, peering through the letter-box, saw a number of letters lying in the small hallway and the receiver of the telephone hanging down from the instrument.

Knocking at the door producing no reply, he went into authority. "Unlock the door, Mr. Stevenson," he said. "I'd better investigate."

Nothing was seen amiss in the hall beyond the dangling telephone. A bedroom which opened out from the side of the hall square was also in perfect order. At the back of the hall another door was shut.

"That's the lounge door, Constable," Stevenson explained. The constable opened it, stepped into the room — and stopped. Turning back he faced the caretaker. "You'd better not come in, sir," he said. "Would you go to your flat quickly and telephone the Paddington police station. Ask for the C.I.D. to be sent here."

"Is Mr. Taylor — ?"

"Dead? . . . Yes. Hurry, please."

Detective-Inspector Gatti with a sergeant and a detective constable reached the house within a few minutes. The inspector looked at the body lying on its back near a settee. The front of his shirt was bloodstained, and blood had seeped over the carpet, leaving a large, ugly stain. Gatti looked at the constable.

"Just as I found him, sir. Nothing has been touched."

"Good," Gatti said. "Now, how do you come into this? You're Aaronson, aren't you?"

"Yes, sir." He told of the street accosting by Stevenson, of the caretaker's anxiety over the uncollected papers etc., and of his decision to enter the flat though he had no warrant to do so.

Gatti gathered up the papers and sorted them out into dates; "Looks from the earliest papers as though he was killed six days ago," he said. "Probably in the evening."

From the caretaker's flat he rang the homicide squad at Scotland Yard, a call that brought Commander Doctor Manson, Chief Detective-Inspector Kenway and Detective Sergeant Barratt of the Squad, and Inspector Thompson with cameras and a fingerprint man.

"Just as the constable found him, Commander," Gatti said. He described the circumstances that had led the constable to enter the room.

Doctor Manson knelt down by the side of the body and subjected it to a cursory examination. "Shot through the heart," he said . . . "Blackening round the area and some tattooing . . . scorching — "

"Which would mean, Doctor, that the gun was held within the flame throwing distance of the nozzle."

"Correct, Kenway. That and the

blackening and the tattooing would suggest that the gun was held at a distance of from three to six inches from the man. Where's the gun?"

"No sign of a gun, Commander," the local inspector announced.

Removal of the man's shirt revealed the entrance hole of the bullet to be circular in shape, and not elliptical. "Fired from directly in front," Doctor Manson remarked . . . "direct confrontation. All right, I've finished here. Get the body away, and ask the Divisional Surgeon to get into touch with me about the *post mortem*. Keep his clothes in a cellophane bag."

With the body of Taylor on its way to the mortuary, the detectives began an examination of the room. It contained as its chief furniture a desk with drawers down each side of the knee-hole. Kenway opened each drawer in turn. The contents of them all were in complete disorder. "Everything has been rifled through, Doctor," he called out. "Somebody was looking for something . . . for what?"

"Something Taylor was engaged on, I should think" — and looked a little startled. Something that Old Fat Man had said a few days earlier sprang into his mind. Half an hour later the examination of the room was completed. "No fingerprints anywhere except those of the dead man, Doctor," Prints reported after he had checked what prints he had found with those rolled off the fingers of Taylor before the body was taken away.

"Then we'll lock up this room, and seal it," Manson said.

"What now, Doctor?" Kenway put the question.

"We're paying a visit, Kenway."

The Doctor's Rolls-Royce purred its way to Kensington and pulled up at a house. The maid who answered the ring and inquiry said: "The family are at lunch, sir. If you would wait — " Doctor Manson pushed her back into the hallway. "Where is the dining-room?" he demanded; and the girl pointed. Followed by Kenway, the Doctor opened the door and stood in the entrance. Mr. Worth rose to his feet. "What the hell?" he began and then recognising his visitors broke into a fury. "Really, this is intolerable," he shouted. "Not only are we badgered at all hours, but now have to face intrusion during our mealtimes." He moved towards them.

"Sit down," Manson said; and the authority in his voice and bearing overcame Worth. He sat down. "I want to talk to Miss Worth." He crossed to her chair. "Now, Miss," he said, "was the private detective you engaged a man named Danny Taylor?"

"I'm not telling the police who he is, not for anything — " she began.

"All right." Doctor Manson turned to Kenway. "Detain her, Kenway, and take her to Scotland Yard for questioning."

"What's this all about?" Worth demanded.

"Obstructing the police in the

execution of their duty. That will do for a start."

Worth stood up. "You'd better tell him, Mary," he said.

"Yes, it was Mr. Taylor," Mary said.

"Is that of sufficient importance to come storming into the dining-room of a private house and try gangster tactics?" Worth demanded. "I will see that this gets to the Commissioner."

"If murder sounds sufficiently important to you, Worth, then it is. We have just found the man Taylor shot dead in his office — murdered. He was apparently getting too close to the murderer of Johnny de Frees." He turned again to Miss Worth. "When was the last time you heard from Taylor?"

The girl had slouched in her chair at the doctor's announcement, and looked on the point of fainting. Her mother went to her with a glass of brandy. "Drink this, darling. It will settle you," she said. "And then tell the police anything you can."

"I'll say what she tells the police," Worth broke in.

"You are wrong. *I'll* say how much she tells me, and how and when — unless you have some reason for secrecy," Doctor Manson said, coldly. "Now, Miss Worth — the last you heard of Mr. Taylor."

Colour returned to her cheeks as she sat up and spoke. "The last time I heard from him was on Saturday night," she said. "He telephoned me at that time. I had told him always to ring, at eight o'clock."

"Did he give you any idea of how far he had progressed in his inquiries on your behalf?"

"No, sir."

Doctor Manson thought he detected an air of restraint in her reply and her manner of it. He probed further. "Well, what *did* he say, Miss Worth? It could be very important for us to know. He is dead, you know."

The girl appeared distressed. She

swallowed hard and put a hand to her mouth. Then: "He told me to pack it in, that's the phrase he used. Said it was dangerous, and he was getting out and was sending my money back." She looked close to tears before, after a slight pause, she went on again. "Then he said there was a man. Then I heard the sound of a scuffling and a noise as if the telephone receiver had been dropped by him. After a minute or two I asked the Exchange to get me the number, but she said the caller had gone away."

"Have you had your money back?"

"No, it hasn't come yet."

"It won't come, Miss Worth. Taylor was killed that night at the telephone. I am going to be brutal, young woman. This man's death lies at the door of your wilfulness. You were told by all of us to leave the tracing of Johnny de Frees's murderer in the hands of the police. Through your studied rejection of the advice a perfectly inoffensive man trying to earn a living has been murdered for a crook like de Frees. It is lamentable conduct on the part of an uncontrollable chit of a stupid girl."

"I'm sending her to Spain, Commander," Worth said as he accompanied the officers to the door. "I have to tell you in confidence that it is because she is to have a child by de Frees — and I want it away from home."

"You will be doing nothing of the sort, Worth. She will be wanted at the inquest on Taylor, and, if anyone is arrested, at the subsequent trial."

"Is there any hope of tracing the man, Commander?"

"At the moment, nothing. But we have hardly begun."

Worth returned to the dining-room in a furious temper and rounded on his daughter. "See what you've done, you bloody little bitch. You were ordered by me and your mother to have nothing to do with de Frees. You go on seeing him. You were ordered not to engage any private detective, and you did. Get upstairs, and if I find you leaving this house without either your mother or me to watch you, I'll thrash you, baby or no baby. Don't you see, you damned fool, that you're likely to be killed yourself for anything Taylor may have told you?"

"That's what Oliver told her," Mrs. Worth reminded her husband. "Oh, dear . . . oh dear." She burst into another flood of weeping.

Worth walked from the room and into his study, banging the door behind him. He sat down to think in front of his desk.

13

CURIOUS murmurings were passing from mouth to mouth in London's underworld. And there were some very odd stand-stills among a section of its denizens. Superintendent Jones, wandering around West End haunts came back to the Yard, and scratched a puzzled head. "Cor stone the crows," he said. "I don't get it."

What Old Fat Man didn't get was the carefree conduct of a score or so of men. They were hovering in their usual haunts, drinking, dicing and gambling in casinos with, apparently, not a care on their shoulders.

They should have had . . . It just wasn't natural.

It was pretty well known that the private eye, Danny Taylor, had been hunting for the killer of Johnny de

Frees. He had, for instance, told Scotch Jock; and, in his cups, his questions had shown other members of the Fraternity the lines on which he was moving. It had been pretty widely believed that Johnny's death came at the hands of the second group of two gangs that had been preying on firms in the city of London, through raids, robberies and other forms of mayhem. It was also known in gang haunts that the £10,000 haul of the de Frees's men had been lifted after Johnny's death — an achievement greeted with some ribaldry. Diamond cut diamond was an apt comment. It was a good story to pass round — an expensive and dangerous daylight raid, skilfully carried out, a fortune snatched after long and brilliant planning, and then lost to rivals in a simple midnight visit after the death of its custodian.

It should have been evident that de Frees had been removed by rivals and his fortune stolen by the same people; and the underworld applauded, originally, the Kilburn public house raid, assault and battery in revenge for the loss of the money.

When Danny Taylor began his probing on behalf of Miss Worth, unwisely among their ranks, seeking as he put it a *quid pro quo* for services he had rendered them — his bending of the law had not ended with his leaving the Force; he could still inform on the Records and the police patrol arrangement — he was met with bland ignorance of any knowledge of the murder. If they needed advice, which they didn't, it was given to them in the Nite Lite Club by Claud 'Gentleman' Sutherland, who was accounted a scholar by his confrères. He advised, *Bouche serrée mouche n'y entre*; and they were very fly in their acceptance of it.

What was worrying the *cerebellum* of Jones was this: after any killing, or major coup, there had always been an exodus from London of those scoundrels looked upon by the

Crime Index with suspicion as having by *modus operandi* some part in it. They remained away for so long as was considered safe; and by their return had established an alibi that the Yard had always found it impossible successfully to dispute. Such operations cost money, but then money, as a poet has said, can move trees.

Jones found it impossible to accept the idea of the presence of suspects in two murders going normally about their business, prepared to talk about the killings as though they hadn't a care in the world, except to find a way to gain illicit means. They went round their usual haunts, played their usual card games, drank their usual drinks and consorted with their usual woman. Whereas, in other days the appearance of the fat superintendent in any bar frequented by them after any crime would be followed by a general exodus of certain people who appeared to have remembered important business so suddenly that they left their drinks unfinished on the bar; on the present occasions they not only stayed put, but waved him a greeting.

It was a peculiar tribute to Jones that though he was one of the most efficient of the Yard 'catchers of men' — the A.C. always held that he was the most efficient — he was regarded with affection by the crooked men of London. He had worked among them for thirty or more years, talked their own language, had sat with them and played games with them. 'Gentleman' Claud was a cardsharper of the highest order, particularly on the Atlantic liners. Jones could, and had, outstripped him to the delight of the underworld watchers. As a confidence man Jones could charm money out of a miser. Fat Man could have made a fortune as a crook — and he knew it. His *bonhomie* with the law-breakers was shared by them to him; and wrong-doers apprehended by the fat superintendent had never borne him any malice; they grinned and ejaculated

"Next time, Super", or "Do you next time, Fat Man", the latter a term of affection in the Yard, and also in the dark areas of the underworld. It was a cognomen in which he rejoiced, with much quivering of his fat.

It took, therefore, a lot to puzzle Jones; and he was at the moment in a state of mither; 'all of a mither', a description he had picked up from his mother, had never forgotten and still used.

There was another odd circumstance calling for surprise; though the Fraternity would applaud any kind of successful outrage on society and keep silent about the operators — and they generally knew their identity — there was among them a unanimous revolt against murder. Few leading criminals carry guns; the last thing they want is for the police to be armed, also with guns.

Consequently, in the case of murder in the Metropolitan area, there is invariably a hint passed on anonymously to the Yard to point detectives in the right direction; and nothing is put by them in the path of detectives who may work on the hint. Now, two murders had been committed, and the underworld was silent. Not a whisper abroad, and it was going about its business, untroubled.

Having turned these facts over in his slow-moving mind, Jones waddled his eighteen stone up to Doctor Manson's study on the top floor of the Yard, next to the laboratory, and poured out his troubles to the Homicide Chief.

Doctor Manson listened to the result of his deliberations, and regarded him curiously. Jones was a man who thought very slowly, possessed little imagination, but when he had at last thought out a problem, he generally had some solution to it; and any idea of the fat superintendent, the Doctor knew from experience, was something to be regarded very thoroughly.

He passed his cigarette case over, chose a Sobrini for himself, and lit both smokes. Then he sat back in his chair, his eyes deep sunk in their sockets, and his fingers tapping a light tattoo on the arms of his chair.

"And what are you trying to deduce from this?" he asked.

"I reckon we've bin a bit out in our suspicions, Doctor," was the reply. "I reckon we're like the girl in the song — we've took the wrong train."

"And landed in a jam, eh? What is your idea of the right train, Mr. Porter?"

"I'm wonderin' whether the killings had anythin' at all to do with gang warfare; whether there isn't somethin' personal behind them."

"On the grounds that nobody in the Fraternity is showing any anxiety, eh?"

"Just that, Doctor."

"But, Fat Man, who would want to kill a very unimportant private eye? What has he to do with it?"

"He hadn't in the natural order of things. If he had been peering into a gang coup, I reckon a warning would have been enough, or a beating up — he had one of those three years ago when he got too inquirin'. No, what I'm thinkin', and it's only thinkin', is that personal shindy over somethin' necessitated the removal of Johnny de Frees. That would have been the end of the matter, only Danny Taylor began to get too close to the bumper-off and had to be stopped from talkin' either to the Worth dame, or to us."

"So!" Doctor Manson was about to comment when Jones stepped in again. "Another thing about it, Doctor, supposin' whoever it is went to the gangs to carry out the death sentence — there's a lifelong danger of blackmail."

Doctor Manson nodded. "True enough. But, if the gang didn't organise it, who did?"

"That's the 64,000 dollar question. I dunno. But did you ever hear of Murder Incorporated?"

"The American organization in crime? — yes."

"Remember they had an executioner, always called on to do the killing?"

"Yes, Anastasia, wasn't he? And you think . . . ?"

"That whoever had a down on de Frees called in a stranger to do the trick, someone we don't know in our crooks' register."

Doctor Manson thought it over. "Sounds like straining a bit, doesn't it?"

"Depends on the importance of the security wanted, Doctor." He leaned forwards. "We don't know the identity of the boss of the Circle lot, the gent who telephones, and types out instructions for robbing and other mayhem, like a ruddy general in the army. That's funny when you come to think of it. Most of the big noises like it known that they are the big noise. Suits their ego. But not this laddie. Even his own crew don't know him. He's a toff and talks class — that's all they know of him. I'm supposin' now. — Right. He's a big man — in business . . . has clubs . . . place in social circles, you might say. Making a nice packet out of crime — we know what the Circle have lifted. What happens if he is found out? Ruddy ruin. Well, de Frees gets through to him. Threatens him. So he has to be removed. But it can't be done by the boss's own men. Chance of blackmail again, see. So he hires an executioner."

"From outside the country?"

"I reckon so, or one who chances to be visitin' us."

Doctor Manson carried the idea to the A.C. "Better get the Special Branch to see if we've had any crooked aliens over here lately," the A.C. said.

14

THE inquest on Danny Taylor held two days later provided nothing to aid the investigations into his death. The chief witness, apart from the doctor, was Mary Worth, who was accompanied by a solicitor engaged by her father. The coroner, apprised beforehand of the girl's connection with the death, said: "I believe, Miss Worth, that you were the fiancée of a man named John de Frees who was murdered by some persons unknown."

"That is so, Mr. Coroner," said Mr. Phillips, her solicitor.

"And I understand that you, unknown to your parents, engaged the services of the deceased Danny Taylor to investigate the circumstances of de Frees's death?"

"To find his murderer, sir."

"Why?"

"Because I did not think the police

were making any progress into the death of my fiancé."

"Really! Had the police, then, taken you fully into their confidence in the inquiries they were making?" There was no answer.

"When did you last hear from Mr. Taylor?"

"On the Thursday night before his death was discovered." She related the evidence of the phone call with its subsequent silence. It was greeted with murmurs of astonishment in court.

"Did you think, Miss Worth, that the noise you heard before the line went dead, may have been a shot?"

"No. It was not a sharp sound, rather a dull thud. I thought that he had dropped the receiver."

"And before that he told you he was quitting, that there was danger, and then added, 'there is a man'?"

"Yes."

"And yet, in spite of this, and the talk of danger and there is a man, you did not report anything either to your parents or the police?" She again made no reply.

Police evidence was given by Superintendent Jones, who said the police were making inquiries in certain directions which he was not at present able to disclose.

A doctor stated that the shot had entered the heart and death would have been instantaneous. The gun, he estimated, had been held a distance of not further than eighteen inches from the man when fired.

Summing up, the coroner said that the girl Worth seemed to be a very wilful person, badly in need of discipline. Her attitude against the police, resulting in her engagement of Taylor had undoubtedly led to his death. He recorded a verdict of murder.

After the inquest, Worth's solicitor, Mr. Phillips, with Mr. and Mrs Worth and their daughter sought an interview with the Assistant Commissioner at Scotland Yard. He said that Miss Worth had been greatly upset by the double tragedy and was in a serious state of health. Her parents wanted her to go to Spain to recuperate away from scenes associated with the death of her fiancé.

Doctor Manson and Superintendent Jones, called in, were critical of the suggestion. "We have two murder investigations on our hands, A.C., both connected with this girl," the Doctor said. "When we make any advance in the inquiries, we will undoubtedly want to question her, and she will not be available . . . "

"You can always see her in Spain," Phillips said.

"Really! Can you explain why we should go to the expense of sending men over to Spain to see her?" the A.C. protested. "There are plenty of places in this country where she can resuscitate in comfort and privacy."

Superintendent Jones looked an inquiry of the A.C. and received a confirming nod. He turned to the girl. "Now, Missee, Mr. de Frees came down to Saxon Hall on the day of his death. Why?"

"He came because I invited him," Worth replied for her. "I wanted to see at intimate quarters the kind of man my daughter wanted to marry."

"But you told us, sir, that you had made inquiries about him, and that he was an Italian gigolo. You knew what kind of a man he was."

"From my inquiries, but only inquiries. I thought that by meeting him I might be able to dispel them."

Jones continued. "Now, Miss Worth, that I understand was the last time you saw your fiancé. You said good night in the hall of the hotel. What were the last words he said to you?"

She replied: "'Don't worry. Everything will be straightened out. I will telephone you from London'."

"I see." Jones nodded his head. "Everything will be straightened out. There had, then, been an argument?"

Mr. Worth chipped in. "There had been a discussion, sir, between the man and myself. I should think there would be discussions on ways and means between the father of any girl and the man she is proposing to wed."

"Accepted," Jones admitted. "Have you got all this down, Barratt?" The Homicide Squad secretary had been told to record the dialogue. He now signified that he had done so.

"Well, A.C.," Doctor Manson intimated, "I think that with her evidence at the inquest on Taylor and what she has now answered in regard to the death of de Frees, we can allow Miss Worth to go Spain, on condition that we have her address there, and that should circumstances warrant it, we can fetch her back here again."

"I am renting a furnished flat at Benidorm, near Alicante," Worth said. "I can give you the address now, together with the telephone number."

They left by air the following morning on a B.E.A. plane bound for Valencia, where a car had been arranged to meet them to take them on the two-hour run to Benidorm.

Within a week there developed what certain Yard officers had forecast following the death of de Frees and the public house fracas at Kilburn — a rivalry between the two gangs who had preyed on London for many months. It began in a small way. Mr. Alexis Constantopolis, a Greek who had lived in London for fifteen years, ran an eating house popular with people of limited incomes situated in the Tottenham Court Road. It carried the name 'The Intimate Restaurant', and served a good middle-class luncheon and dinner with four courses for eight shillings and sixpence. Its thirty-five tables were generally occupied, especially at night, when there were often two sittings.

As he was cashing-up after dinner on a Tuesday night a boy appeared in the entrance, and on being accosted handed over an envelope addressed to Constantopolis. When opened it spilled a card on which was printed the following information:

MUTUAL INSURANCE ASSOCIATION

The above association offers to
....
(Here the name Intimate Restaurant was filled in in ink)
complete security against robbery damage to premises and furnishings, and regular and safe deliveries of all foodstuffs, in return for a modest premium.
If Mr...
(again the name was filled in in ink) will put an announcement in *The Times* within the next three days, with the initials A.C. and the word 'agreed', a representative of the Association will communicate with you.

P.S. This offer lasts only for three days.

Constantopolis, on his way to the restaurant next morning, called in at the Tottenham Road police station and asked for Inspector Apperson. To him he showed the card. "Ah," the inspector said. "You know what this is? The Protection racket. Going to put the ad. in *The Times*?"

"No," Constantopolis replied. "I'm asking you to stop it. I'm already protected, see."

Asked to explain the latter remark he said he had a friend with influence who held a dinner card which entitled him, and anyone else showing it, to free meals in the restaurant. It was an arrangement several years old.

"Then what is all this about?"

"I don't know. That's what I want the police to find out, and put an end to it."

"What about that friend of yours who gets his eats in return for his influence?"

I haven't seen him for several weeks. I guess he's away somewhere."

"What's his name?"

"Signor Gina Fattorini. He's Italian but has lived here for years."

"And you haven't seen him for some weeks." The inspector stared at him for a minute, thinking. Then: "Is he a sallow, tall, thin man with black wavy hair, very much oiled? And did he wear a gold wristwatch?"

"Yes, that's him. You know him?"

"I've seen him around. Well, leave this card with me, Mr. Constantopolis and I'll look into it."

With the restaurant owner gone, he hurried with the card to Scotland Yard. Superintendent Jones was, at the moment, the sole occupant of the Homicide Squad. He listened to the story of Constantopolis and looked at the card. "Lor' lumme," he said, and growled. "I suppose everybody's handled the ruddy thing . . . no ruddy prints . . . but we'll try it." He sent it up to the Fingerprint Section of Records, then crossed to a filing cabinet and came back with a photograph. "This

174

Fattorini?" he asked.

"No idea, Super. I've never set eyes on him that I know of. I'll show it to Constantopolis and — "

"No you ruddy well won't. If this is a protection racket, and I'll lay a hundred to one it is, an' a copper is seen goin' into the place, Constantopolis's number is up. I'll get one of our girls to go in there for a cup of coffee and let him see it and say whether it's Fattorini. And it's a pretty good bit of work for you to bring it along here, Apperson," he said condescendingly. "You had an idea?" The inspector nodded. "Just a vague suspicion, Super. I might have been wrong . . . might still be."

An hour later the girl returned went into Homicide and announced: "Mr. Constantopolis says the man in the picture is Mr. Fattorini, Mr. Jones."

"Ha," Jones said, "I reckoned he would." He telephoned the Tottenham Court Road police station. "Apperson?" he said. "Say, you struck oil."

Doctor Manson who had sat through the incident, looked across. "And what, may I ask, is all that about?"

Jones told him of the card offering protection, and the fact that he already was in with protection through a friend Mr. Fattorini, and didn't want any other.

"I see," the Doctor said, but didn't see at all! "And who, may one ask, is Mr. Fattorini?"

Jones chuckled. It sounded like the rumblings of thunder in the distance. "He ain't anybody, Doctor, but he *was* Johnny de Frees."

The Doctor sat up, suddenly, and looked hard across at the super. Jones nodded. "Yeah, sure, Doctor, we're in trouble. It's on, laddies, it's on. De Frees as Fattorini — and I reckon that was his real name — was 'protecting' the Intimate Restaurant not, apparently, for cash but for free meals for himself and his gang. That, you will know, was only the Intimate. He was working protection over the manor. Now, with him gone, the Red Circle have moved in on his manor — an' the de Frees lot ain't goin' to sit down and lose their pocket money."

"Why have they been allowed to go on with it — over years you say?"

"Shucks, Doctor, you gotta have evidence. An' how many people payin' for protection are goin' to tell the police about it, and get their places shot up?"

The Assistant Commissioner issued orders. A police watch was to be kept on the Intimate Restaurant, plain clothes men from another division, who were not likely to be noticed in the vicinity. After telephone conversations, Mr. Constantopolis agreed to engage a night watchman to patrol the premises after closing hours. The burglar alarm direct from the restaurant to the police station was to be tested last thing after closing, and a police patrol along the road was increased.

No advertisement went to *The Times*. The time limit on the card expired on the Saturday — with nothing untowards happening. Saturday night came and went, and Sunday dawned. Sunday luncheon was a slack time in the Intimate, but for the night dinner hours the place was crowded. The last meal was served at ten-thirty o'clock, and the doors were shut at eleven-fifteen, when Constantopolis left after seeing that everything was in order and the alarms were working. From then on, the night watchman, installed, was under orders to telephone the Tottenham Court police station every half-hour reporting all peaceful.

He so reported at two-thirty o'clock and said, jocularly, that he was going into the kitchen to fry himself an egg. At two-thirty-eight the road was startled by a loud explosion. Police cars were on the spot within minutes, and *walked* into the restaurant through gaping doors.

The interior of the eating house had been blasted into absolute ruin. Tables and chairs had been blown into pieces, the mirrors that lined the walls were shivered into nothingness, and debris lay over everything.

Members of the Special Branch, called in, gave it as their opinion that the explosion had started at a spot in the centre of the restaurant room. Mr. Constantopolis said that that spot had been occupied by his cold table, which was one of the best in town. It was always covered with a damask cloth which hung down almost to the floor on all sides. "Ah, then, that's it," a Special Branch man said. "The bomb could have been shoved under the table, and hidden by the cloth."

"What size would it be?" the inspector asked.

"Oh, quite small, really. Most of the damage is due to its explosion in a confined space, you see. I should say it was set to go off at two-thirty o'clock. We'll probably find traces of the mechanism when we go through this stuff."

"What kind of holder?"

"Oh, almost anything which wouldn't be noticed. Could be a handbag, or more likely a cardboard box which could have been shoved under the table by the foot of a diner."

"There were diners in front and at the sides of the cold table," Mr. Constantopolis said.

A demolition squad began clearing-up operations, and Mr. Constantopolis wended his sad way homewards.

15

"THERE'LL be some more," Jones said. A discussion group was gathered in the Yard, the topic of which was the blowing up of the Intimate.

"How come?" Inspector Apperson asked; and there was a twitching of his face as he put the question. The disaster was in his manor, and if there were more to come then he and his staff were in for a busy time.

"Because this was a warning, laddie — 'See what happens when you don't play ball' intimation to all and sundry. Got any hotels in your manor?" he asked, knowing full well that there were half a dozen of them.

"Yes . . . Good God, you don't mean — "

"Blow 'em up? No, too bloody costly and too risky. It'd be killin' the goose that's goin' to lay the golden eggs. But don't kid yourselves, any of you. Things are goin' to move. Rackets are profitable these days when there's plenty of money about. They're easy money, cos folks are scared too easily. In the Yew-nited states umpteen billions of dollars a year are spent by the citizens in protection. What's a good racket in the U.S.A. must be a good racket in England, or France, or Germany or anywhere else you like."

"The law . . ." began the A.C. Jones snorted. "The law! How are you goin' to expose it. Law! We gotta street betting act. It's agin the law to bet on the streets or in a pub. If a fellow's pinched he's fired, or mebbe goes into stir. And yet a million or so changes hands every year on the streets in the pubs and gaming houses."

"But there's been protection here for years. We know that, but we haven't been able to stop it because . . ."

"Nobody'll say they're payin' . . ."

"Yes, but why should it be busting

out more now, Fat Man?"

"Bah! Up to now it's been peanuts. De Frees got free meals. He also had about twenty places who paid him a hundred or two to stop hooligans who weren't hooligans at all but his own men from making trouble in the cafés and dancing places. Then there was a kind of gentleman's agreement — if you'll pardon the expression — between the two sets of bastards not to poach on each other's preserves."

He laughed. "Come to think of it, they were more honest about the agreement than most business houses who are respectable folk. Now, with the boss of one gang gone for keeps the other lot are free to move in. They ain't out for peanuts. Look, they've got cards, printed cards, advertising their goods. Printed and all ready for names to be written in. That's the Yankee way." Jones had spent three months in New York and Chicago as an observer of their brand of crime and detection.

"See, what will happen — just as

happened to the Intimate. A card will be handed in to one of the classy hotels . . . "

"We'll ask them to give us the tip and we'll . . . " said an inspector. Jones laughed. "Don't be a bloody fool. D'ye think they'll tell you if they receive one? They receive the card, and what do they do? A payment of five thousand nicker would be chickenfood compared with what damage the gang could do to the place . . . "

"You said there wouldn't be violence," Apperson protested.

"Not material violence, son. Have another look at that business card. 'Safe delivery of foodstuffs'. An army marches on its stomach and a hotel marches on other people's stomachs. You stop that, or muck about with it and the number of stomachs will begin to dwindle. Reputation makes or breaks hotels."

"Doctor . . . " the A.C. began. The Doctor sat up. He had been leaning forwards, his hands cupping his chin.

He appeared to be meditating, and made no response.

"Doctor!" the A.C. called again.

"Eh? You want something?" He came to sudden life.

"Your views . . . " The A.C. began again. Manson waved him aside. "Begone," he said. "I don't know why you dragged me in here. I have no interest in Constantopolis or his Intimate Restaurant. They fall not into my circumspection. I am homicide. You are — well, *denuntiantem ne supra crepidam sutor judicaret*, Edward."

"What's he say?" Jones whispered. "Let the cobbler keep to his last," Kenway translated. "He says protection is nothing to do with him."

"I'm only interested," the Doctor went on, "insofar as the impression seems to be that these occurrences are fostered by the people who may have disposed of de Frees and are now raiding his grounds. That's the theory, and all I can say is why have they suddenly blossomed out into protection

185

when they've had one half of the West End for years and haven't so indulged before?"

"On the principle of live and let live, I reckon," Superintendent Morrison said. "The bosses were prepared to share the manors out. Then one of them dies and the leaderless are floundering. Wouldn't *you* jump in and seize the opportunity?"

"Mebbe," Manson agreed, "but I've got two murders. I wish you every success. Come along, Jones." They walked out of the room.

"I gotta an idea," the Fat Man said when they had regained the Homicide section of the Yard.

"That being?" the Doctor asked.

"Tell you when I get back." He waddled out. In the street he made for a telephone kiosk, and called for a number. To the answering voice he said: "Get down there, pronto."

It was two hours later that he reappeared and entered Homicide chuckling. Part of the interim he had spent in conversation with Detective-Inspector Ainslie who is in charge of that section of the C.I.D. employed in keeping observation to prevent and detect offences.

That officer kept an unobtrusive watch on a club in Pimlico and had a squad car in close readiness should it be required. The club was frequented by a variety of men, mostly of dubious character, but had always been run in accordance with the law for that very reason.

An hour or two after Ainslie's precautions a fracas broke out in the club. Detectives entering forcibly found a hefty fight in progress. Chairs were being used as weapons, together with a bottle or two. A couple of men were lying semi-conscious on the floor behind the bar; one a barman who had been unwise enough to attempt to stem the row — he ought to have had more sense. The upshot was that Ainslie's men arrested Alfred 'Whizzer' Burns and 'Scotch Jock', carted them to the police station, where the desk sergeant accepted a charge of disturbing the peace and engaging in a fracas in a public place. They were accommodated, by prior arrangement, in separate cells well apart from each other.

Superintendent Jones saw them separately, also by arrangement, in the cells. With his baby face set in seeming concern and in his beguiling voice, he addressed Burns. "Cor lumme, Whizzer (the word means pick-pocket) what in hell's got into yer," he commiserated. "Dammit, you know the dicks are watchin' yer. Why in hell do you want to get into a push-up like that?"

"They wuz moving in on our living, Super. And they wants our nicker."

"But, Alfie, they got that — ten thousand nicker that you lifted from Durands."

"There's more'n that, Super. That was the last lot." Jones smiled to himself. Burns had now admitted taking part in the raid. But, he argued, there was still no evidence that could be brought in a court of law.

"I know all about that, Alfie. It's hooked away an' you has ter 'ave Johnny's signature to get it out, an' he's dead and gone. Where in blazes is it, Alfie?"

"Ah, that'd be tellin', wouldn't it?"

"Listen, Alfie, they're goin' to wipe out your protection racket. That's what you mean by saying they're movin' in on your livin', ain't it?"

Alfie nodded.

"Who are *they*?"

Alfie shied away. "Look, guv'nor," he said, "I ain't planning to have a knife in me back in some quiet street."

"Sure . . . sure, Alfie. It needn't happen. This is between you and me. I ain't never split on anythin' I've been told, and you know it. Now, if we can knock 'em off, you've got your livin' back. That's sense, ain't it?"

Alfie, after earnest thought, and

somewhat against his better judgement, spoke four names.

"There now," Jones said. "We've suspected them. And the Boss?"

"You kiddin'?" Alfie burst out. "You'll have to ask them for that. And they can't tell you, see, 'cos they ain't got no idea."

"Cor, Alfie, we know about the telephone calls — " the man looked a little staggered at the extent of the police's knowledge — "but supposin' they do get orders out'a the air, as you might say, somebody has to be top cat in carryin' them out. Who?"

"Well, guv'nor," — he gave the matter some reminiscent thought — "as I seems to remember it's Scotch Jock who tells them to come or git."

Scotch Jock in his cell wasn't so helpful. "Hop it, bogey," he said when he saw Jones entering his cell. "Hop it."

"Cor stone the crows, Scotch, it'll be you that will be hopping it if you keep gettin' in the hands of the police. The boss won't like it, you know. I kin pass the word that you've talked a little bit — and it'll be all up for you. What in hell made you go and rough up Johnny's lads for money you thought they'd put away? The boss ain't interested in pennies. Or was it your own little idea to make a bit on the side? Boss keeping the grand up his sleeve too long?"

Scotch began to whistle. Jones gave it up.

He was back with Alfie within an hour. "Take a dekko at this," he said. "It's a list of places which I know have been handing out money for protection by Johnny." Alfie cast an eye over the names, and looked somewhat staggered. "Didn't think we knew, eh, Alfie?" Jones said, and grinned. "Now tell me, how much of your livin' and the livin' of the mob has gone up the spout, 'cos of the Circle boyos?" Burns stayed silent.

"Wot, all of it?" Jones commented

on the silence. "Lumme, you'll all 'ave to go on Public Assistance, or do a job o' work."

Jones carried his gathered *coups de dupe* to Inspector Ainslie, just as Doctor Manson walked into the inspector's office for information on the arrests; and he listened to the Fat Man's recital with astonishment. "How the deuce . . . ?" he began; and was interrupted by Ainslie sitting back in his chair and howling with laughter until tears ran down his face. He sat up, wiped his eyes and panted. "He'll be the death of me one of these days, Doctor," he said, referring to Jones. Manson rubbed a bewildered hand across his forehead.

"How come?" he demanded.

"He fixed the ruddy fracas at the club, Doctor, and had us standing by all ready. Engineered the whole bloody thing. We had to look for two people he named — one from each side. Now see what we've unearthed."

Doctor Manson looked at his superintendent.

"How, Fat Man?"

"Oh, shucks, it was easy. I got me 'canary', Snoopy, to go for a drink in a pub where Scotch Jock goes and pass on a whisper he said he'd heard that Johnny's boyos was sharin' out some of their doings in the club in a back room in the afternoon at three o'clock. Then Snoopy whispers to Johnny's boys that Scotch Jock is goin' with his mob at three o'clock to collect protection from the club, which was always Johnny's province. I told Ainslie here of the arrangement for us to join in."

"I see." Doctor Manson frowned. "I thought I told you, Jones, that I wanted no part in the protection racket, but had two unsolved murders on my hands . . . "

"Sure, Doctor, but the Circle crowd put Johnny away as you believe an' I was after the unknown boss. He's the killer we want."

"And how does this exploit help in that?"

"Shucks, Doctor, we've heard that the mob don't know his identity, except just a voice over the telephone. A voice who to? Somebody has to see that instructions are carried out pronto. Well, now, me little arranging lands 'Whizzer' Burns in a cell where I sees him and tells him they're goin' to lose all their living. I shows him a list of places where Johnny's lads had been drawing protection money, and I gathered that he and the others had been round them and had been told there was no more gelt for them, meaning that the Circle boys had moved in. He's flaming mad because of the fight and all, and tells me under the rose so to speak, that he don't know who the Boss of the crowd is, just like the others don't know, but the bloke who gives the come-on and get-out is Scotch Jock."

"In other words," Ainslie said, "the

phone calls we have heard about go to Scotch."

Doctor Manson nodded in realisation "Yes, I see," he said.

"I've given certain instructions, Doctor," Ainslie closed the conversation.

16

DESPITE all the efforts of the homicide staff, investigation into the two murders was still hanging fire. Several weeks had elapsed since the body of Johnny de Frees had been disinterred, by accident, from his lonely grave; and three weeks had passed since the shooting of Danny Taylor. That the two tragedies were connected seemed to be in doubt by reason of the interference of Mary Worth. But any reliable evidence to that effect was lacking.

Forensic examination of the office in Portobello Road disclosed that there were no fingerprints anywhere except those of Taylor himself, and a number identified as those of Miss Worth, scattered on the surface of the desk on the opposite side to where stood Taylor's chair. The telephone earpiece had been wiped clean of all marks.

Papers from the disordered drawers and files had been separately tested piece by piece without any success. People who rented adjoining offices, questioned, said they had seen no strangers about: except for one woman who stated that a young woman had paid several visits to Taylor's room. From her description it was evident that the young woman in question had been Mary Worth. Nobody had heard any shot. Since the shooting had taken place after eight o'clock at night, that was not surprising; most of the offices were closed by six o'clock.

There was the same absence of evidence attending the killing of de Frees where, again, there were no fingerprints to afford any clue. The deserted Oldsmobile, which had the most promise of prints, was useless. Not only were the registration plates fakes, but the licence was also a forgery; and the chassis and engine numbers had been filed off. Not that this mattered a great deal because infra-red rays and the spectroscope had easily revealed the numbers in the depth of the casing. There, however, help faded out. The car was fourteen years old, had been sold originally to a Nottingham garage, and by them to a customer. This man, seen by the police, explained that he sold it privately after three years to a customer who paid him cash. Examination of the records showed that it had passed through a number of hands since. Its last owner was unknown.

In short, in neither murder was there anything to go on save deduction, and that on a doubtful basis. Doctor Manson began to doubt the dictum that 'murder cannot be hid long'.

Alone in his study he collected the dossiers of the cases, together with statements gathered from outside sources and settled down to concentrate on a new examination. "There must, just *must*, be something I have overlooked," he muttered to himself.

Poring over the dossier of de Frees, he turned to the evidence of the girl Mary, and of Worth. De Frees and Worth had gone for a long walk alone. The Doctor's reading of the evidence given at the inquest seemed inconsequential. He studied intently two statements appearing in the dossier. ONE: Worth said he had invited de Frees down in order to see what kind of a man his daughter wanted to marry. Yet, later, he had said that he knew the man to be an Italian gigolo. Then, why did he invite him down to Saxon Hall? If it was to discuss relations and a possible marriage to his daughter why did not the talk take place in her presence? Why take a walk with him? TWO: What was behind the girl drawing de Frees aside in the hotel hall when he was on the point of leaving and behind his remark overheard, and subsequently repeated to Superintendent Jones during the discussion on whether she could be permitted to go to Spain? De Frees had said to her, "Don't worry. Everything

199

will be straightened out. I will phone you from London in the morning." But he was apparently dead by the morning — and buried in the distant grounds of the hotel.

What had Worth said to him during that walk? How came it that de Frees after that walk had never left the hotel grounds? And whence came the Oldsmobile car? Where was de Frees's Austin Princess car which he always drove? Not a trace of it could be found, not even among the Fraternity who made a practice of disposing in a variety of ways stolen automobiles.

For a time he (Doctor Manson) had looked with suspicion on Worth himself. There were good grounds for it on the surface — the walk, the remarks of de Frees on leaving: what was to be 'straightened out'? the accompanying of de Frees to the hotel entrance in speeding the parting guest. On investigation, however, all suspicion in that direction had had to be abandoned. He said himself that he saw de Frees leave the hotel entrance and turn towards the car parking space, and a minute later heard a car drive towards the road. The secretary and the hall porter corroborated that. The gardener, returning from the village pub, said a car passed him as it emerged from the drive. Mr. Worth also said that after he had closed the hotel front door he went into the hotel bar and stayed there until he went up to join his wife in their bedroom. There were a dozen people to confirm the fact. He was given a cast-iron alibi, and that had to be recognised.

A very odd circumstance next occupied his attention. The girl said that she had met de Frees in the Nite Lite Club, where she had gone because an old schoolgirl friend said it was 'an entertaining place'. He turned up an account of an interview with Mary Worth. De Frees, she said, was in the club with two men on her first visit. They were together at a table. When the men left he came across to her table, asked if she were a new member and could he share the table as he 'never liked being alone'.

It was obvious that he had forced an acquaintance on the girl. Why? He probably knew her identity from the schoolgirl friend; and also the identity of her father, a wealthy man and in business as a financial adviser and consultant. He was probably then well aware that she was an only child and her father's heiress. Was that the reason for his forcing an acquaintance? The Doctor thought it most likely, in that case, that he had asked the schoolgirl friend to get Mary into the club in order that he could meet her, with her fortune in view, and within a few weeks had become engaged to her. According to Mr. Worth, Mary had said that de Frees told her he was a successful business man.

It was, the Doctor realised, an oversight on his part not to have obtained from Mary the name and address of her friend in order that she could be investigated. It could, possibly, still be arranged.

The greatest puzzle in the case was the murder of Danny Taylor. Why should a private eye's inquiries into the death of de Frees necessitate his removal? Nothing in the two cases seemed to make sense.

Worth appeared to have nothing to do with de Frees's death. Yet, when Taylor sensed danger — heaven only knew from where — it was Mary Worth he warned and advised to take no further part in the inquiry into the death of her fiancé; and in doing so, met his death.

The A.C's theory, and that originally of Jones, was that he was killed by a rival gang who subsequently lifted ten thousand pounds obtained by de Frees by robbery, and had the idea that there was more hidden away. Hyams, the lawyer, had the idea that de Frees might have told Mary Worth where that hoard was secreted. If de Frees had, indeed, done so, then the girl was indeed in peril — if the murder had been carried out by the rival gang.

Against this was the fact, promulgated by Jones, that the gang was going about its business in spite of murder inquiries by the Yard — a most unusual proceeding, and a dangerous one.

Sitting back and reviewing the dead end position of the investigations, the Doctor communed, mentally, that he required the thread of Ariadne to unravel the mystery of the two deaths if the investigation were not to end in the way of the task of Sisyphus — that is, never solved. He put away the dossiers and wandered into the Strand to the Dilettantes Club for tea and cakes. Sir Edward Allen, the Assistant Commissioner, seeing him in the doorway beckoned him over. The club, lately removed from almost its ancestral home into the busy West End contained only a sprinkling of members; the majority made appearance only at the lunch and dinner hours, and at the card table period.

The A.C. eyed the sombre appearance of his chief executive. "No light, Harry?" he suggested.

"None. Listen — " He went over point by point the conclusions through which he had struggled in his study for a couple of hours. "That is the position, Edward. What do you make of it?"

Sir Edward leaned back in his chair — a roomy club leather nest — and fitted the monocle on its black riband into his perfectly good left eye, an idiosyncrasy whenever he was troubled, and after a pause spoke. "What does Jones think of the situation? Is there anything in his suggestion that there was something personal about the death of de Frees? Might that account for an association between the two killings?"

Manson grimaced. "Jones!" he ejaculated. "I'm damned if I know what he is up to. He seems to be wandering between the Scylla of Protection and the Charybdis of murder, with the apparition of Nemesis in the distance."

"And you don't see any connection?"

"To be quite candid I do not. In any case what has the protection racket to do with him?"

"It has something to do with me, Harry. I'm in the position of Janus, you know — looking both ways. Come along. You can give me fifteen and I'll beat you at billiards."

17

THE Hotel Magnificent is situated in the most select, and the quietest area of London's West End. The name, florid and bombastic though it may appear to sensitive minds, is in fact, without exaggeration, justified.

The Hotel Magnificent is, indeed, magnificent, from its front door to its roof garden, which latter gives a spectacular view of London including in its panorama a glance into the gardens of Buckingham Palace, and the Green Park.

The caravanserai is comparatively modern, being only some fifteen years old. Alabaster pillars hold up an artistic portico leading into the building. Inside, the spacious hall (the description seems hardly adequate) is lined on two sides with elegant miniature shops, offering expensive jewellery, gifts, ladies' modes in the current fashions, gentlemen's tailored fashions, a ladies' hairdressing salon and a gentlemen's tonsorial (not barber, please) shop.

Behind all this are Sauna baths, a gymnasium for both sexes, and in a garden at the rear a heated swimming pool, with instructors. The main lounge walls present surfaces of quilted ivory satin from ceiling to within three feet of the floor, the latter space being lined with maple wood. The chairs and lounges are of ivory-coloured leather.

A ballroom accommodating 100 dancers is similarly decorated, except that instead of quilted ivory satin it is of quilted ivory kid leather. Two dance orchestras in the ballroom are augmented by a third playing soft music in the lounges, and during meal-times in the restaurant. And there is a cinema.

The restaurant is lined on all sides with floor-to-ceiling mirrors. Snow-white napery is graced with silver cutlery and cut-glass.

Upstairs, the word bedroom is never mentioned, only suites. Each suite has an entrance hall, which can do duty as a small sitting-room, opening into the bed chamber. Each has a bathroom and toilet, a telephone, a radio and, in the more expensive first-floor suites, a nine-inch television set. Hidden lighting in all sections of the rooms are controlled by a battery of press buttons alongside each bed.

There are reception rooms for private parties, dinners, etc. From top to bottom the entire hotel is carpeted in thick pile of various colours to suit the décor. Thus, it will be recognised, that the hotel is, indeed, magnificent.

So are the prices. There is a minimum of fifteen guineas a night, breakfast additional. A week's stay in one of the cheaper suites will lower your bank balance by some £75. If you are desirous of making a splash, then a week's stay and entertainment can cost you anything up to £250.

Nevertheless, the hotel is invariably full. Americans, crowned heads of Europe, and notabilities from central Asia form the basis of its clientele. Meals are described by connoisseurs as 'out of this world', a circumstance due to the presence of several *cordon bleu* chefs. Luncheons are sixty shillings and dinners five pounds ten shillings without wine. Water is, however, placed on the table free of charge.

On the particular evening when disaster struck the Magnificent there were just over a hundred clients sitting down for dinner. The restaurant manager, Signor Guiseppe Carmenetti (an Italian, of course, since Italians are far and away the best restaurateurs) was receiving diners at the entrance, and chatting with regular customers whose faces were familiar to him.

The menu was of the usual high standard comprising (in French, of course):

Turtle Soup
Fillets of Sole Mornay
Fillets of beef, with potato garnish
Cauliflower with white sauce
Roast Chicken   Lettuce Salad
Viennoise Pudding
Cheese Fritters
Cheese
Dessert

Soup was brought from the kitchens by Commissar waiters (white-aproned) in tureens and served at tables from a heated trolley. Turtle soup, the real thing, not mock turtle which so often hides under the name of turtle, was a speciality of the Magnificent and was partaken of by most diners.

It was not until the chicken was due to be served that anything unusual happened. Then, however, several diners left the table stating that they felt unwell. Then, within a quarter of an hour, pandemonium reigned over the room. Diners everywhere either sprawled over tables or bent double in their chairs, holding their middle. A dozen or more were making a dash for the toilets. Women all over the place were screaming.

When doctors, hurriedly called, arrived the dining-room presented an appearance more like a field dressing station than a hotel restaurant. They rendered first-aid to the less affected sufferers; others were put into hurriedly summoned ambulances and carted off to hospitals.

Those diners able to explain their symptoms complained of extreme stomach pains, colic and diarrhoea. Among the doctors was a Harley Street specialist. He shook his head at the recumbent diners. "It looks to me like some form of poisoning, but I can't say until I have examined the people," he said, "but were I you, I would call in the police."

"Poison!"

A now nearly demented manager called the police. A superintendent of 'A' Division, hearing the Harley Street man's suspicions, telephoned Scotland

Yard. Chief Detective-Inspector Ainslie, picked up from his home by a Squad car, heard in outline what had happened.

"Right," he said, "leave the restaurant just as it is, tables and all. Lock all the doors and give me the keys." That signalled the end of the five pounds ten shilling dinners for a hundred or more people. The inspector also impounded the kitchen from which the dinner had been served.

It was not until after the early hours that pathologists, testing the contents erupted from stomachs, and probing the ailing parts of the victims, announced that the collapses were due to an irritant poison, in all probability, Tartaric Acid. Further tests were needed to confirm that, but that there was poison was undoubted.

Now, Superintendent Jones first heard of this hullabaloo when he reached the Yard at ten o'clock on the following morning. Told the bare facts, he said, "Ha! . . . Ha!" and left the Yard.

Ten minutes later he entered the Magnificent and waddled to Reception. "The manager," he demanded.

"I'm afraid he's very busy just now, sir. Will . . . "

"The manager . . . pronto," Jones repeated.

"I'll see . . . "

"The manager!" Jones roared. And when an angry or frustrated Jones roared, it sounded like a male lion on the track of a meal.

He was shown into the manager's office. "What can I do f . . . " the manager began.

"How much?" Jones asked.

"Pardon?"

"How much?"

"Really, sir, I don't understand. And I'm very busy . . . "

Jones went round the desk and seized him by a lapel. "Listen, you ruddy Wop," he said, "don't . . . try . . . ter . . . kid . . . me." (In between shakes). "This ruddy . . . hotel . . . 'as been . . . poisoned. How . . . much

214

. . . did . . . they want?"

The manager swallowed hard. His face turned a pasty colour. "Five hundred a week," he confessed.

"Got the letter . . . the card?"

"No, it was over the telephone."

"Ha! Well, laddie, you'll be hearin' from 'em again. An' you'd better pay — until we catch 'em. Else they'll want the ruddy hotel next."

"How much did you pay the last lot?"

"There wasn't any other lot, Superintendent."

"I get it . . . too risky . . . too big for 'em."

He waddled back to the Yard.

"I said it," he announced in the A.C's office. It sounded like a paean of triumph.

"Said what, Fat Man?"

"I said as there'd be more protection when they moved into Johnny's manor. He was small beer; this lot ain't."

"If it *was* protection, Jones," the A.C. doubted.

"Five hundred nicker a week they wanted." He told of his conversation with the manager. "Told him to pay in future," he concluded.

"You *what*?" The A.C. nearly shot out of his chair.

"Told him to pay. Only way. Gives us time to track . . . saves his hotel."

★ ★ ★

Pathologists investigating the foods in the hotel, traced the poison source. It *was* Tartaric Acid, an irritant, but hardly fatal poison affecting the stomach. It had been mixed with the soup. And every diner had taken soup. The tureens contained traces of it and so did the cauldrons in the kitchen from which the tureens were filled for transmission to the restaurant. Everything else, the fish, beef and chicken were cleared. "Too difficult to get it there," a pathologist explained.

The head chef fainted when told the bad news, and had to he brought round with brandy. "But, gentlemen," he moaned to the investigating officers, "we don't have any Tartaric Acid in the kitchens. How on earth *could* it get into my soup?"

"Yes, how?" Inspector Ainslie asked.

"Put in by somebody in the kitchen, laddie," Jones said.

"We'll have them all up. Turn them inside out. I'll . . . "

"Forget it, son," Jones said. "Forget it. The hairs of your head are numbered, according to the good Book, but you can't count 'em. There are forty men in those damned kitchens, all told, and what is one among so many?"

Fat Man was right. The kitchen staff and the waiters were vetted, and eyed by men familiar with faces and with long memories, but no arrests were made.

"We'll have a watch kept on hotels," Ainslie said. "Anything even mildly unusual, and we'll arrest on suspicion."

"Don't waste public money," Jones advised. "There won't be any more."

He giggled. "Clever bloke, the Big Noise. He was usin' psy . . . psych . . ."

"Psychology, Fat Man?" Kenway suggested.

"That's it, Kenny. And they'll 'ave learned. They'll pay up on demand. The boss . . . the Big Noise — take your pick — is goin' to collect thousands of nicker in the new manor."

"How is it going to help us, Jones, in murder?" Manson queried. "That's our problem — *and yours*," he said, pointedly.

"Watch, Doctor, and see who's blewing nicker. They'll have plenty to blow. And when we see the blewing — that's the mob we want."

The A.C. nodded. "Patience, cousin, and shuffle the cards till our hand is a stronger one," he said, quoting Scott.

18

SUPERINTENDENT JONES'S dialogue with 'Whizzer' Burns, duly related to Doctor Manson and Inspector Ainslie, and which demonstrated that 'Scotch Jock' was the mouth of the problematical and elusive Boss, had elicited from the inspector the comment, "I've given certain instructions"; and those instructions had been approved by Doctor Manson.

"Forget everyone else and concentrate on Jock," the inspector ordered. "I want him tailed constantly as far as is possible. There are four of you he won't know because your regular duty is outside the West End. Never let the same man trail him more than once in the same session in order to avoid a chance of recognition, and change your clothes and appearance."

"Anything to note specially, sir," one

of the company asked.

"Yes, a telephone. If he should go into a kiosk or a telephone anywhere pop in at once afterwards and ask the operator what number was asked. Use Scotland Yard to get a reply, if you have to.

"Now, he hasn't got a telephone in his lodgings so he has to go outside to send a message or to receive one. I reckon that there is an understanding that he rings up a certain number at a given day and time and receives instructions. And I'm damned certain that somebody rings him also at a given number, probably three times a week.

"Now listen. This is protection *and murder*. If any one of you falls down on the job through his own mistake I'll have the coat off his back. Should anyone ask what job you're on tell them to go boil their heads."

"Suppose he phones from inside a building or a club, where we can't enter . . . "

"That's arranged — the club I mean.

I've got a stooge inside."

It had been easy. There was a petty thief in the membership of the Nite Lite who had become one of Inspector Robbins's 'narks'. It was arranged that he should break into a house in a side road at Shepherd's Bush — and be caught in a room. Hauled in front of the magistrates, he was sentenced to seven days after receiving a packet of notes from the inspector. The circumstances of the break-in were reported in the papers.

His appearance in the Nite Lite on the eighth day, swearing horribly against the police was greeted with derision. "Look at the ruddy burglar," shouted Boxing Jim. "Why the hell did you go and break into a dick's house? Off your ruddy head?"

"How did I know a dick lived there. I sees a window a little bit open at the bottom. I knocks at the door and there was no answer, so I nips in. When I hears the front door key, I hops out again, and a bloke collars me." It was accounted a good joke and worth drinks to the victim. It also removed any suspicion from him.

The manoeuvre brought results, but not the one hoped for. Several scraps of talk overheard, landed two malefactors in trouble before they had completed their operations. Scotch Jock did not use the telephone at all.

Several days passed away without any development that Doctor Manson could co-relate to Johnny de Frees or Danny Taylor. Then, one of the tailers of Scotch Jock saw him enter the end one of a bunch of telephone kiosks. He nipped into the fourth — the most distant one from Jock and rang. To the exchange he said: "Miss, a Scotland Yard officer here. A call is being made at this moment from another kiosk here. I want the number that caller is asking for. If you are in any doubt of me, record the number, tell your supervisor and I'll get an inspector to ring you from the Yard." The girl, with commendable wariness did just that. Ainslie rang the supervisor, identified himself. "The number recorded, sir, was NOT 0627," the supervisor announced.

The combined efforts of the Information Room failed to trace the number. There was no number NOT 0627 listed in the Directory. Through the offices of the Postmaster General the name of the ex-Directory subscriber and the address were obtained. It was a woman, a Mrs. Aimee Burroughs, of Flatlet 4, at No. 13, Normandy Road, Notting Hill.

"A woman!" Ainslie said . . . "Good . . . A front for someone. We'll root her out, pronto."

"You will do nothing of the kind," Doctor Manson chided. "I'm in this in front of you . . . murder. You send your men clambering all over the place and that's the last we'll see or hear of it. Leave it until after midnight, and we'll let Kenway go along and see what he can find out . . . "

Kenway did! The described flatlet

was hardly a flatlet in the accepted sense, but rather a large room above suites of offices. From a bunch of keys Kenway selected one or two before finding one that opened the door of the room. Standing alongside the wall at the side, he pushed the door wide open with a foot and waited . . .

There was no movement or sound from inside. He walked in.

And stopped dead, in surprise.

A cloud moved off from the face of the moon and with a myriad stars in the sky combined to light up the room sufficiently to show that it was practically bare of furnishings. "Good Lord!" Kenway said. He pulled a heavy curtain across the window, and making sure that no gleam would be seen from outside, switched on the light.

And stared round.

The room's only contents were a table standing in the centre of the floor, and a plain wooden chair set alongside the table, and that was all.

"Who the hell can live in here?" he

communed with himself, in whispers. "No stove, no domestic utensils, not even a cup for a drink of water. No bed."

The table held a telephone with an attachment for receiving and recording telephone messages in the absence of the owner. With a gloved hand, Kenway wound the tape back, and switched on the recorder. After a pause a voice came over:

"Please record your message, and speak slowly and distinctly."

There was a further pause and then: "It all went okey-dokey, Boss." Then silence again, and although Kenway waited several minutes, there was no further message. Carefully, he wound the recorder back.

Doctor Manson and Inspector Ainslie listened next morning to the results of Kenway's investigation. "You didn't by any chance recognise the voice?" Manson asked.

"No . . . no . . . but — "

"Describe it as best you can."

Kenway imitated the depth and texture in the words.

"Scotch Jock for a tenner," roared Jones, who had joined the trio.

"That's it," Kenway said. "There *was* a kind of accent . . . and a burr in the voice."

"What was 'okey-dokey' do you reckon?" Ainslie asked: and answered his own query. "The Magnificent, of course. There hasn't been anything else."

"That we've heard of — as yet," Jones countered.

"Well, we've established one thing — the telephone from which this Boss — if what we've been told is correct — sends out his orders, and obviously at which he can be reached by his men, or by one of them," Manson said. "We ought to be able to do something about that."

"But — a woman!" Ainslie turned an idea over in his mind. "*Could* it have been a woman, Kenway, with a deepish voice?"

"Search me. But I don't think so. The timbre was wrong to my mind for that."

"If the 'okey-dokey' meant the Magnificent, then . . . "

Doctor Manson grimaced. "No, Ainslie," he said. "NO. Forget that. You won't find any of the Boss's men were anywhere near the hotel. This man's clever."

But the Yard tried. They had the names of four men whom 'Whizzer' Burns had provided under pressure from Superintendent Jones. All had alibis that did not even need testing.

Later, the superintendent made the rounds of shops, cafés, etc., whom he knew had paid in cash or goods to Johnny de Frees for protection. All were in sound working order and reasonably prosperous. "I reckon the gang is raking in a couple of thousand a week," he reported. "And" — this with a wry smile — "they ain't spending much of it at the present — while the heat's on."

19

OCTOBER in southern Spain is perhaps the most enjoyable month of the year for *extranjeros*. The sun has by then lost that devastating 100-plus degrees of heat and humidity of the summer months, and its searchingly penetrating rays have lessened. If this is so of southern Spain generally, it is amplified in the resort of Benidorm, for the five or six miles of deep sandy beach, through the long sweep of a bay is wide open to the sun. There are no rows of hotels practically on its front; hotels there are, but singly, not in battalions, and lying back from the wonderful Levante beach of white sand.

The October temperature is in the neighbourhood of 75 degrees, shining continuously from a deep blue sky. For this reason the resort is popular with the English, both as a holiday resort and as a winter residence from the rain, snow and cold winds of Britain.

Five or ten minutes' walk inland will bring the visitor to the old village — it can hardly be called a town — with its attractive buildings, shops, delightful cafés and restaurants, and an excellent English library kept by an elderly Englishwoman, and with modern British fiction. A short bus ride takes visitors to Alicante where there are cinemas.

Access to Benidorm is easy to those who do not fancy the long two-day train trek via Paris and Madrid to Alicante, and then a bus or drive to Benidorm. In the summer months a plane flies direct from London to an airport at Alicante; in the autumn and winter months a B.E.A. or Spanish plane goes daily to Valencia, whence one can train or bus to Benidorm.

Furnished luxury flats are available, not so cheap as they were once — the tourist trade has ruined cheapness in

Spain — but still within reach of the reasonably well-to-do citizen during the winter periods, and of considerably better accommodation than a good many furnished flats in Britain's resorts. The Spaniards of Benidorm are a friendly people, honest and with a penchant for *los Inglesi*.

It was in a flat in a luxury block situate centrally in the length of the Levante Beach that Mrs. Worth and Mary were installed, and in which they occupied the pleasant days, lounging on the balcony in chaises, or laid on the warm beach in the sunshine beneath sun umbrellas during the daylight hours, and in the evening sewing small garments in preparation for Johnny de Frees's child.

Johnny, however, was never mentioned between them. Ellie Worth was too depressed by the disaster to her daughter to talk about it; Mary Worth, deprived of a father for her child, and shadowed by her part in the death of

Danny Taylor kept her thoughts to herself.

Her mother received daily letters from Worth, asking what progress was being made about the child, and emphasising on her the need to have it adopted by some English family, or a Spanish woman; he did not want, he said, the child brought back to England where the fact of his daughter's *mesalliance* would, by its presence, become public property, and in so doing hold him up to derision.

The idea was opposed by Ellie Worth who, like all women with children, welcomed the idea of a grandchild to fuss over, and hoped when the infant arrived, to talk the matter over and persuade him to let them 'adopt' it.

Meanwhile they had made a number of friends, both British and Spanish, and enjoyed entertaining and being entertained at home and in various restaurants.

Thus, life was being passed in pleasant dalliance — until a night towards the end of the month. On that night the two were sitting over a late cup of tea, having returned from a visit paid to a friend in a neighbouring block of flats. It was just after eleven o'clock. Benidorm at that hour is on a par with the deserted village of the late Mr. Goldsmith. It was with some astonishment, therefore, that their peace was disturbed by a ring at the flat door.

"Who on earth can that be at this hour?" Mrs. Worth said. "You aren't expecting anyone, are you, Mary?"

"No, of course not, Mother."

"I'll go." Mrs. Worth switched on the hall light, unlocked and opened the door. A hand from someone unseen in the darkness pushed her back into the flat, while another hand clapped over her mouth. A second man closed the door and switched off the light.

"Who is it, Mother?" Mary called from the lounge.

"Two old friends, ducky," said one of the men, and pushed his way into the room, holding Mrs Worth by an arm. Mary looked up, and put a hand to her mouth. The unwelcome visitors she recognised as the two men who had been with Johnny on her first visit to the Nite Lite when he crossed over to her table and asked if he might join her.

"W . . . W . . . What do you m . . . mean, p . . . pushing into the flat like this? W . . . what do you want?" she asked.

"A little talk, dearie. Just a little friendly talk — and nothing will happen to you. Johnny was killed. You know all about that. We were Johnny's lieutenants, so to speak, in all his jobs.

"Johnny was the banker. He kept the loot until it was safe to divvy it out — all except what you might call our spending money. See? Well, now, Johnny's gone. Only he knew where he cached the money for safety. We knew where the last loot was — in the safe at his flat until he could carry it away in safety. It was pinched — ten thousand quid. But we don't know where he put the other stuff, thousands and thousands, which belongs to us. We worked for it, and we want it. Now, be a good girl and talk. *Where is it stacked*?"

"Me? . . . I don't . . . k . . . k . . . know anything about it."

The men looked at each other and swore. "Going to be difficult about it, are you?" one said. He produced a rubber cosh. "Look," he said, "we don't want to get nasty, lady. It's taken us a hell of a time to find out where you were. Ran out, did you? I'll . . . "

"She didn't run out from anywhere," Mrs. Worth said. "We came here because she is going to have Mr. de Frees's baby, and she isn't married. We came to avoid our relatives."

Number two sneered. "O.K.," he said. "She's going to have a baby. Johnny seemed to be acquiring quite a family. Only, you see, you're different.

He was going to marry you; he wasn't marrying any of the others. Now he wouldn't have had any secrets from his light of love, would he? So where's the doings?" He produced again the cosh and waved it. "This is what Johnny persuaded people with. And we are good persuaders — always were." He made a pass at her with the cosh.

Mary Worth stifled a scream and put a hand to her stomach, and Mrs. Worth stood in front of her, facing the two men. She said: "Now, you listen to me. Mr. de Frees told Mary he was a business man in a big way. She believed that, and so did I. It was not until after his death — his murder — that we knew what he was. The police told us. He was *after* Mary's money, not to *give* her any. She's been doing her best to find the man who murdered your friend, though he let her down very badly.

"If she knew where any of de Frees's money was, she would tell you, and so would I, because neither of us wants to have the least association with him any more. We don't know anything about his money. Now get out, and find where it is from his friends. If you have come all this way under a misapprehension, then I'm sorry, but we don't know anything about it.

"My daughter has money of her own and her father is a rich man, and she will inherit what he has. Why do you think she would want to have anything to do with her fiancé's money?"

"He told me he had a big business and plenty of money," Mary chipped in.

Number one raised the cosh again and clipped her across the shoulders with it. "There'll be more coming," he said. "Where is it?"

Mary Worth moaned. "You can kill me if you like," she said, "and I still won't know. Go on, kill me. It might be the best way out for me."

The man hesitated. Number two pulled him away. "Look," he said, "she's going to have a kid. I reckon she don't know, like she says. I reckon Johnny never told her nothing. Let's get out. We don't want no killing, not here in Spain.

"O.K., lady, we'll be watching you. If we find you've been playing games with us, my God, I'll cut you into little pieces, me and the other boys. And don't reckon on calling the cops when we've gone, see."

They left. Mrs. Worth locked and bolted the door and went back into the lounge trembling in every limb. She found Mary unconscious on the floor. Rushing to the telephone she called frantically for the doctor. Doctor Gomez took one look at her and telephoned for an ambulance. In the early morning she was admitted to hospital in Alicante.

Norman Worth arrived by air twenty-four hours later, having received an urgent telephone call from his wife: "Come here at once, Norman." He heard from her the story of the midnight visitors, and the result.

Two days later Mary Worth had a miscarriage. Mrs. Worth dissolved into tears. Worth took a philosophical view. "It is probably for the best," he said. "It solves all our difficulties. You can both come home when she is fit to travel. See how right I was, Ellie, when I said I wouldn't let her marry that bloody rogue? Men from the Nite Lite she said, did she? I'll contact the Yard when I get back."

"I shouldn't do that, dear," she urged. "You'll get her killed or something."

Worth, back in London, had second thoughts, and let the incident lapse.

In fact, he did little of anything but sit in his club and go into a dirge of self-pity. Everything, he thought, was going wrong. There was the estrangement from his wife over his refusal to countenance the marriage of Mary to de Frees; the discovery of the man's body in the grounds of the hotel where he had visited him (Worth) and Mary; then again, Mary's wilfulness in rejecting all advice and engaging a private detective, and the subsequent publicity of inquest and police inquiries; and finally the death of the detective for which the Worth family were blamed.

He would have gone away, possibly abroad, except for his business organisation which held him in London. He considered whether it would not be wise at this stage to give up business altogether and live quietly somewhere in the seclusion of the country.

At ten-thirty o'clock, he donned a dark overcoat and hat and went out into the darkened streets.

20

CRIMINAL detection is not the easy arm-chair detection of the fiction writers; it may be described as eighty per cent hard routine and slogging, ten per cent deduction, and ten per cent sheer luck. So far in the Johnny de Frees and Danny Taylor murders, the Yard officers had endured the slogging, had had little fortune with the deduction, and no luck at all.

Until now.

The modicum of luck now apparent lay in the discovery of the room at Normandy Road, Notting Hill. The Yard men were not too sure about its occupant — obviously from their acquired knowledge, the Boss, referred to by that description in the underworld, but not known by name; the mysterious figure who telephoned instructions and sent scripts of planned operations.

"Mrs Burroughs!" the A.C. said . . . "a woman."

"Well, A.C., women *have* been gang leaders before now," Inspector Ainslie reminded him. "There's nothing against a woman."

"There was 'Diamond Annie' who ran the 'Forty Elephants' round the Elephant and Castle," Jones waxed reminiscent. "They ran a protection and blackmail racket led by Annie. There was Moll Cutpurse, and Constance Kent and Ruth Synder, and a gang of shoplifters who planned wholesale raids and shared the plunder. Lumme, don't let a woman worry you."

"You think the Boss is a woman, Fat Man?"

"I dunno, but I don't dismiss the idea."

Now, set a woman to catch a woman is accepted by Scotland Yard as a sound maxim. The A.C. gave it a go. Detective Sergeant Freda Adams was called in. Jones said she seemed ideal for the job, being an attractive looking young woman, with a businesslike air about her when in plain-clothes. She dressed for the part in a neat dark business suit and a close-fitting cap over her brown hair. Jones briefed her; and to Notting Hill she went in her disguise as a canvasser for a new local business guide and professional reference book.

At number thirteen she mounted to the top floor and rang the bell of flat four. No answer being forthcoming she knocked hard at the door, which was locked. She then made her way downstairs, calling at each office and talking shop. Her final question to each of the occupants was: "Do you know when I can catch Mrs. Burroughs at number four?" Her report when she arrived back at the Yard was, to say the least, unsatisfactory.

"Nobody, sir, has ever seen a woman go up to number four. Everybody thought the flat was untenanted since no occupant has ever been observed there or going up and down the stairs."

"No men?"

"No men, either during the time that the next door and underneath have been occupied."

"Which means," Jones said, "that the recorder is visited at night."

That night after midnight, Kenway visited the flatlet for the second time and wound back the recorder. "Please record your message," it said . . . and after that there was silence. The silence persisted for three succeeding nights following the usual instructions to record any message. On the fourth night, however, there came in the same voice as formally the laconic report, "Seen and read and understood." Kenway carried the information back to the Yard.

"Something's in the wind," Jones prophesied. "Keep at it, and we'd better have a watch."

It wasn't difficult. At a request from the Commissioner of Police the manager of Messrs. F. W. Filey Ltd., business transfer agents, presented a key and permission for an officer to spend one or two nights in their office after the hour of darkness. "We want to keep observation for a rumoured arranged raid on the offices of the bookmaker across the road," he was told.

The office was situate half-way up the staircase, so that anyone proceeding to number four would have to pass the door of Filey and Co. Kenway kept vigil in the dark, ears attuned to the slightest sound. As daylight dawned he mounted to number four, wound the recorder back and waited.

Silence greeted the action.

The message of the previous night had been erased.

He made the announcement when he reached the Yard.

"Dammit to Hades . . . he got in." Jones swore.

"Listen, Fat Man," Kenway looked annoyed. "Nobody went up those blasted stairs. I had the door slightly ajar. A ruddy mouse couldn't have run by. I'll swear to that."

"Then there's some other way in." Jones looked across at Ainslie. "We'd better get busy. There's something about to move."

If there was, it was something the immediate underworld knew nothing about, or even suspected. Ainslie's 'nark' in the Nite Lite, called to their secret talking place, insisted that there was no nervousness such as is usually apparent when some move was in the offing. The members were going about their ways with apparent unconcern, drinking and gambling.

Jones's 'nose', Snoopy Pitman, had heard no whispers, he said, talking out of the side of his mouth when they met as strangers in the public house over a glass of beer.

"Cor stone the crows, it ain't nacheral," Jones said. "What in hell has got into 'em? Ain't they got no pride any more?"

And so a week passed away with no more incident than a street bashing, a robbery or two, and the hundred and one offences which occupy the police every day of the week.

Watch was kept unobtrusively on the premises in Notting Hill, and Kenway paid nightly visits to the room, but without any satisfactory results. Nobody was ever seen to enter number thirteen other than those known to be employed on the premises.

London was quiet from a criminal point of view; no hotel or restaurant incidents occurred in the West End. Even Soho seemed to have reformed itself.

* * *

Now, with the new industrial era of the trade unions there has come about many changes in national industry — some authorities say changes for the better: others regard it as for the worse; it all depends on the point of view. These changes seemed to have worked out on the lines of more pay for less work; less production per man power for higher wages, forced by unofficial strikes: regarded as a right by one class; viewed by others as providing the necessity for making a signed agreement between unions and firms constitute a legal document and contract similar to that as between a private employer and an employee, the breaking of which constitutes a breach of contract which can result in the award of damages. Since there has been a minimum of never less than two unofficial strikes a week (sometimes three and four) over the last twenty-nine months, throwing thousands of people who want to work out of employment without remuneration, there may be some reason in the argument, especially when the result is to affect seriously the country's export trade.

One important change in the industrial situation is the payment of wages, salaries, etc. In days gone by they were paid as the workers left the factories on Saturday morning; later, with the five-day week, the paying out took place on a Friday evening. With the arrival, more or less of a four-and-a-half day week the payment date became a Thursday.

The problem was aggravated by two circumstances: the growth of factories and works all over London area with resultant large increases in the numbers of employees, and the growth of criminal methods of hijacking wages on the way from the banks to the firms' premises; an operation which, if successful, resulted in tens of thousands of pounds getting into the hands of people who had never even worked for it.

This has brought into being a number of security measures. The chief of these is the introduction of security transport, in the form of heavily built and steel-lined vans with uniformed attendants, three or four to each car: a driver and deputy driver in the enclosed cab and two others locked with the money inside the car. Security firms have sprang up throughout the country guaranteeing to move money and other valuables safely from one place to another for a fee.

As wages money was needed for Thursday it is necessary for the firms to receive it on Wednesday evening or early on Thursday morning in order to give the firms sufficient time to work out the amounts and to envelope each man's money in order to pay out in the late afternoon. (In the case of the five-day week the system works a day later).

A further development is the problem of the amount of money for such wages. With the huge growth of employees in certain industrial circles money invariably has to be transferred from a central source to banks in the vicinity of the firms' premises — a double security deal.

This homily brings us to a Wednesday afternoon in November.

21

AT three o'clock in the afternoon a black van bearing on its sides the inscription 'Security Transfer Limited' and no other description, set out from Threadneedle Street on a regulation weekly journey. Its driving seat (enclosed within bullet proof windows) housed the customary two uniformed drivers. Inside the van itself two men, also uniformed, took their places behind the locked rear door. Around them were canvas bags each secured with a seal, and each bearing a label. They were arranged in groups of varying sizes.

This was the usual weekly supply of monies requested by bank branches in order to comply with the demands of various works and factories throughout the areas covered, so that they should be able to pay out wages by the week-end.

The delivery route of this particular van was to circulate the banks in a semi-circular route which took in Finchley, Hampstead and Highgate with a turn homewards towards West Ham. When it starts on its journey the van holds notes, silver and copper to the tune of something over £100,000. As each bank is reached a small trolley is wheeled out from its premises and the necessary bags are taken out of the back of the van, the guard of two men standing by the open door, and accompanying the money to the inside door of the bank to make sure of safety, since a number of cases had occurred where the bags were hi-jacked during the short journey, under the menace of revolvers. Two bank officials, and the manager, remain on duty after the closing hour, to receive, sign for, and lock the money safely away in the bank's strongroom.

The operation was one that had been carried out weekly over many months, in sunshine, in rain and in cloud; and the route was familiar to the two men in the bullet proof glass protected driving cab of the van. This particular Wednesday was in no way different to any other except that rain had fallen heavily during the previous night, and the sky was leaden in hue. By three o'clock rain had started a drizzle again and fog had begun to gather over the river and was spreading inland. As a result it was almost dark when the van started out. Against the greying mist one could see the necklaces of lights winking along the curves of the road. Traffic began to crawl with a firefly glitter, the cars jerking at holdups, and sounding their horns with a weary plaintiveness.

Donald Hodson, the senior driver, saw his load into the van, marshalled his guards inside and locked the door. He looked up at the murky greyness around him. "Going to be a bloody journey," he said. "We'll be late all round. Better warn the customers, son."

"We'll do that," the bank assistant

said. "Not as they won't be expecting it, seein' as they can look out of the window and see what the weather's like." Hodson climbed into the driving cab, pulled the door closed and locked it. The money procession starts.

The first port of call, a bank in Hampstead, was reached half an hour late, and the requisite money was unloaded, carried into the bank, checked and signed for. The journey was restarted, Hodson turning into Hampstead Grove and making his way to a bank on Highgate.

At the junction of North End Way and Spaniards Road, where White Stone Pond is skirted, the van was flagged down by two mobile squad police. Hodson leaned out of his cabin window. "What's up, mate?" he inquired.

"You the van carrying bank money?" a sergeant asked.

"That's right. And we're bloody late with this 'ere fog. Why?"

"Good. We've been searching for

you. The Yard sent out a radio warning that there's a mob out after your doings. A nark let it out."

"A highway holdup! Jees!"

"That's right. We're coming along with you as an extra guard. We'll ride in the van so as to be ready if there's any attempt at a holdup."

Hodson clambered down and opened the van door. "Trouble, you chaps," he said. "These cops are riding with us."

"Welcome to our home," one of the guards said. "What kind'a trouble?"

"Suspected attempt at taking the cash from you. Hi!" he called to Hodson. "What's your name?"

"Hodson . . . Donald Hodson."

"Right. Now look, let's try to avoid any trouble. Leave your usual route where they'll be waiting for you. Take the cut across the Heath and then drop down into Hampstead Lane. They won't be expecting you along there."

"O.K."

The officers stepped into the van, and Hodson locked the doors again, climbed into his cab and set off once more.

The fog had thickened; it always did come down heavy on the Heath and the adjoining Ken's Wood. Visibility was down to a little under fifty yards and Hodson was straining his eyes to follow along the left-hand side of the road, and cursing silently at the slow pace he had to make.

A quarter of a mile along Spaniards Road (which is half a mile long), he jammed on his brakes with a violence that caused the van to lurch. In front of him and directly in his path were two large lights. The lights of a car. "Bloody fool," he said, "what the hell's he doing in the middle of the road in a fog like this?" He proceeded slowly towards the lights, and saw that they came from a car standing obliquely across the road, with a man standing in the roadway in front of it. He stopped and let down his window.

"In trouble, mate?" he asked, and the man came forward.

"Yes. *You are*," was the reply, and was accompanied by an automatic jammed up close to his body hanging out of the cab window. A second man appeared at the opposite side of the van. "Get down, the two of you," Hodson was ordered.

Hodson got down. He was no hero — and neither would anyone have been with an automatic staring him in the face. But before he stepped out of the cab he had given the warning signal of three quick knocks on the rear of his driving seat — an agreed signal to his men inside to be on the alert.

"Open up," the hijacker leader said. Hodson stepped to the back of the van, grinning slightly at the surprise awaiting the men when they would be confronted at the opening of the van door with the two police officers housed inside. As he opened the door he stepped quickly to one side to avoid any contact as the police rushed out.

No police appeared at the open door. Instead, the hi-jacking pair stepped into the van. Peeping round, Hodson saw his own guard lying bound and gagged on the floor inside, and the supposed police joining the hi-jackers with satisfied shouts.

"Get back in your cab and pull the van off the road on the right," the leader of the men said. "And look slippy if you don't want a bullet in your guts." The speaker turned to his companions. "When we're on the grass get the stuff in the car and get away. Just drive naturally. Don't rush things or you'll get stopped by the bogies. You know where to go. The Boss will be in touch. I'll take care of the van. You" — to Hodson — "get inside with your men. And keep quiet so as no harm will come to you. We ain't out for your lives — just the bloody money. Give us a nice rest in the sun, this will."

With the November fog now thicker than ever, there was no traffic along Spaniards Road. It wouldn't have mattered if there had been, for the van and the getaway car had been driven fifty yards over the grass, and the road was not even in sight. The pseudo policemen transferred the money bags from the van to their car, and drove off.

With Hodson and his deputy driver in the van along with the tied-up two guards, and the door safely locked, the leader of the hi-jack team got into the cab, regained the road and drove in the direction of Highgate, taking the Hampstead Lane.

★ ★ ★

The first anyone knew of these proceedings was when, at seven o'clock, the manager of a bank in Highgate telephoned London. He had been teetering round in his bank for hours and was 'all burning hot, in rage and anger high' like the man in Charlotte Gilman's *Similar Cases*. He decided that he wanted his tea and freedom from the bank's premises. So he picked up his telephone and called

258

the headquarters.

"Where the devil is our money?" he demanded. "We've been waiting here since four o'clock and now it's after seven. Am I expected to sit here all the flaming night?"

"Sorry sir, but the fog . . . "

"I know all about the fog, man. But dammit they could have walked with the money in the time."

"There's nothing we can do about it, sir. The van left here as usual at three o'clock. They should have been with you by at least five o'clock, even for the fog."

He replaced the receiver and then had a nasty thought. Taking the phone again, he called up the Hampstead bank. Getting no reply he looked up the address book and telephoned the manager at his home address. A woman's voice answered. "Ah, is Mr. Searle there?" he asked.

"Just a moment," came the reply, followed by a shout, "Alfred, the bank wants you." Searle took the receiver.

"Heavens, man, can't it wait till the morning?" he protested. "What is it? Have I received the wages money? Dammit, of course I have . . . Time? . . . the van got here about four o'clock, a bit late. Is that all? Right. Good night."

"Funny," the bank custodian ruminated. "Why the hell hasn't Hodson phoned if he's met fog trouble? Oh, well . . . " He gave it up.

Not until a West Ham bank telephoned for news of the van's progress did he begin to wonder. "Not reached you," he said, and listened. "Yes, of course, left here at the usual time. I'll look into it."

The time had reached eight o'clock. Now, a little worried, he got in touch with the security people. Security, without panicking, phoned Scotland Yard. "There may be nothing in it but fog trouble," they said, "but you never know. And it's been five hours."

The Yard put out a call for news of the van's progress after it left

Hampstead. There was also a call to hospitals and garages in case there had been illness or a breakdown. The replies were negative.

Morning dawned with still no news. The Yard sent out emergency calls: the van must be found. The fog had cleared during the night. Inspector Ainslie took over the search. He talked with security.

"Where was the last contact with the man Hodson?" he asked.

"Hampstead bank. He was there just turned four o'clock, sir."

At Hampstead the manager reported that conditions there had been as usual. "He was a bit late, Inspector, because of the fog. We carried the bags in and signed for them. Then he left."

"You saw the van go off?"

"Sure."

"Which way did it take?"

"Towards Hampstead Grove — his usual route — on the way to Highgate."

Ainslie telephoned the Yard. "He never reached Highgate," he reported to the A.C. "Something happened between Hampstead Grove and there. I'd like squad cars sent along here and we'll run a search." At the local police station he asked to have all men who had been on street duty called in for questioning. Had they seen anything of the security van during their patrolling?

A police constable replied, emphatically. "Yes, sir, I saw it at about four-twenty at White Stone Pond. It was stopped by a police car and then turned towards Spaniards Road."

"Spaniards Road? What the hell was it doing going up there? Get me the driver and crew of that police car."

"Police car, Inspector?" the local superintendent said. "We hadn't a police car out that afternoon."

That was when Ainslie, and the Yard, became not only worried but alarmed. It was made perfectly clear by the Squad command that no police car could possibly have been in the vicinity of Spaniards Road before four o'clock, or after that hour for that matter. There was no car patrol in the area.

Squad cars arrived at the Heath in a hurry. Led by Ainslie in his own car they drove along Spaniards Road, and along West Heath Road and North End Way. Inquiries proved fruitless. The van had not been noticed in either of the latter. And there wasn't likely to have been anyone on the Heath Road itself in a fog like that of yesterday evening.

First intimation of the van's changed journey was found about a quarter of a mile along Spaniards Road. A sergeant in a police car moving at a walking pace, with the crew scanning the road, called out, "Here, sir." Ainslie drove up and got out. The sergeant pointed to tracks going off the road on to the Heath. "A heavy vehicle, sir," he pointed out. The tracks were followed to a spot some forty yards or so inside the Heath, where they merged into other tracks which mingled, leaving identifiable traces in ground that had been softened by the rain of the night before, and by the moisture from the fog.

Around the wheel tracks were a number of deeply trodden footprints. "Keep clear of those prints," Ainslie ordered. "And you, Dawes, take the car back into Hampstead and get some posts and ropes. We'll rope off the area. Got a car cover in any of the vehicles? Then just cover up as many as possible of the footprints, until we can get plaster casts taken from them."

22

FROM his car Inspector Ainslie talked on two-way radio with the Assistant Commissioner (Crime) and with print men from the laboratory.

The A.C. trotted upstairs to Doctor Manson. Standing in the open doorway, he looked at the three occupants of the room — Manson, Superintendent Jones and Chief Detective-Inspector Kenway. There was that in his face which halted the greeting usually accorded a visit from the head of the C.I.D. Doctor Manson stood up. "What's wrong, Edward?" he asked.

"The bank security car has been hi-jacked," the A.C. said bluntly. He waved a hand in the air.

"Cor!" Kenway ejaculated.

"How much?" Jones asked.

"Something like £50,000 or £60,000."

"Where?" Doctor Manson awaited the answer.

"Half-way along Spaniards Road on the Heath." He recounted all that Ainslie had told him over the car radio. "They want Lab men there," he concluded.

"Fingerprints?"

"No, there is nothing to take finger-prints from. The van has vanished. There are wheel and footprints. Seems probable that the money was transferred from the van to a car at the spot."

"Kenny lad," Jones broke into the conversation. "Get like hell down to that flatlet, or office, or whatever it is called in Notting Hill, and see what's on the recording thing."

"In broad daylight, Jones?" The A.C. looked startled.

"In daylight, A.C. I reckon we ought never to have stopped the nightly visits. Kenway in plain-clothes won't be known as a cop, and he can walk in during business hours as though he were visiting an office there. I think we

266

had better root out Scotch Jock and his cohorts, and I'll want to know where they were yesterday, and they'd better have a damned good story."

On the Heath the Lab boys were busy. "It's the van's tracks all right, sir," Merry, the deputy scientist of the Yard, told Inspector Ainslie.

"How come?" the inspector asked.

"Off-side rear wheel marks are those of a Michelin tyre, and the near-side are Michelin Xs. That's how the van was fitted."

"And the car tyres?"

"Oh, there you have us. They're Dunlops. No help unless we can find a fault in them. We'll take plaster casts and hope for the best. What do you reckon happened?"

"As I read it, the van was stopped, then driven off the road to here and the money transferred to the hijacker's car. There's no other possible explanation. He wouldn't pull up for anybody or anything. Those are bank orders. He was always carrying bank money and there have been too many attempts at robbery from security cars."

"He'd pull up for a police car," Merry suggested, grimly.

"Bent coppers, do you mean? . . . Poppycock. Not even for sixty thousand pounds. Besides, there wasn't a police car out yesterday."

"No, but what about a *purported* police car, laddie?"

"That's more like it. A flatfoot says he saw a police car just short of White Stone Pond at four-twenty, which would be just before the van left the Hampstead bank after delivering cash. It wasn't possible."

The tracks left on the Heath showed plainly that after the mêlée left by feet going backwards and forwards, both van and car were driven a few yards along the Heath and then turned on to the road. What traces remained on the roadway suggested that the van had been driven onwards towards either Winnington Road or Hampstead Lane. The former direction would take it between Hampstead Heath extension and golf course to East Finchley; and the latter to the crowded area of Highgate.

"Probably used the car as a police escort for the van, sir. Safety first, so to speak," a detective suggested.

"No." Merry shook his head. "The car went off first, obviously with the money."

"Evidence," Ainslie demanded.

"The van tracks cut across the Dunlop tyre marks of the car at several places. Obvious."

Back in the Yard, returned from the trip to the Notting Hill room, Kenway showed none of his usual elation at success. In reply to the inquiry in the eyes of Doctor Manson and Jones, he lifted his hands. "Room cleared out," he said disgustingly. "Not a damned thing left. And no fingerprints."

"So," Old Fat Man said, "they've done their last coup — and a big one."

"Come again?" from the doctor.

"Room vacated, Doctor. Recorder gone . . . No more telephone talks from the Boss, see . . . Gang come to an end. I reckon we've been getting a bit too close."

"Ah!" the A.C. said. *Ad Praesens ova cras pullis sunt meliora.*"

"What's he say?" Jones whispered to Kenway.

"Eggs are better today than chickens tomorrow, Fat Man, meaning, in point of fact that they've decided to take what they've got now than possibly lose everything in the future — in gaol."

"Or the Boss has," Doctor Manson said. His sharp ears had overheard the whispered dialogue. "He's the chief loser by the stopping." He made a tent with his fingers, and regarded his subordinates disapprovingly. "I've said before that I have no interest in the Boss and his gang. I'm interested only in a couple of murders. Let the C.I.D. handle the Boss."

Jones shook his head. "Look, Doctor," he said, "whatever else the gang operates, they've something to do with the murders, too. De Frees was killed and a rival mob go all out against the Boss's lot. Why? Dammit, because they knew that the Boss's mob had wiped out their own boss and had taken over his manor. When that private eye gets on to something, he's wiped out as well. It's my reckoning that the Boss, who we don't know, is responsible for the killings, the murderer or murderers of which we also don't know."

"All right." Doctor Manson threw in his hand.

"Get them in and see what you can learn."

Scotch Jock and his cohorts were playing cards in the Nite Lite when Yard men walked past the protesting doorman and into the club. "C'mon, you lot, we want you at the Yard," a sergeant announced. Half an hour later, they were visited in the Interrogation Room. They sat silent as Superintendent

Jones and Inspector Ainslie walked in on them.

"Any trouble?" Jones asked the sergeant.

"No, sir. Came like lambs."

"Finish the metaphor, Sergeant."

"Finish, sir?"

"Sure, son. Like *lambs to the slaughter* — Jeremiah. You should read the Good Book." He looked at Scotch Jock. "Bad . . . very bad . . . " he said, shaking his head mournfully. The four waited. "Never knew you come with the cops like lambs afore, Scotch. What's got into you?"

"Sin' we ain't done nuthin', Mr. Jones, we ain't got naught to face from the dicks. See? So we accepts the invitation."

"Ain't done nothin'. Now, ain't that nice! There'll be joy in the Yard over four sinners that repenteth." Ainslie chuckled at the quip.

"Now, let's see." Jones screwed up his face in a pseudo effort to remember something. "There was somethin' I wanted to ask you . . . Ah, I remember. Had any phone calls from the Boss lately?"

Shocked surprise at the question and the knowledge behind it pulled up Scotch in his chair. "Phone calls . . . the Boss?" he echoed.

"Come off it, Scotch. We know you were the kingpin of the Boss, saw as the orders in the scripts were carried out, and so on. Calling him up and leaving messages on the answering recorder." (The four looked at one another. Jones chuckled at the unspoken message passing between them). "Oh, son, there ain't much we don't know about you. More'n you think. Scotch you had a telephone number to call. And you never knew where the phone is, cos the number ain't in the Directory. But we can tell you where it *was*. In a top room in Normandy Street, Notting Hill. Laddie, we've listened to the recorded messages.

"Here's one, Scotch." Jones lowered his voice half a pitch and spoke. "Please send your message and speak clearly and slowly. It all went okey-dokey, Boss. Recognise it, Scotch? It was *your* voice. Dammit, we've heard your voice often enough to be able to recognise it. That okey-dokey was the do at the Magnificent Hotel. We knew that, only you weren't actively engaged in it, or we'd have pulled you in."

Scotch was staring at him out of wide-open eyes. Jones pushed a telephone over to him. "Ring the number, Scotch, and leave a message. Any message you like. Just any message."

With his eyes still staring, Scotch dialled and waited for the invitation: 'please leave your message'. There was no sound. Jones chuckled. "I said I could tell you where the telephone *was*, Scotch, not where it is. Now listen, you mugs — all of you. Yesterday a bank security van was hi-jacked and sixty thousand nicker taken off it. It went to the Boss to be cached until it was safe to divvy it out. You don't know who the Boss is, only a number which Scotch here knows to ring and you don't, and a number from which orders come from him, with a typed script for each of you to read." (They looked dazed at the revelation).

This morning we were in that room hoping to play back a message sent by Scotch, or somebody else. What did we hear? Nuthin. What did we find?" Jones leaned forward confidentially, and sank his voice like a dramatic actor imparting chilling lines in a play. "We found the room empty, and swept, Scotch. The reply recorder gone, and the tenancy, in a woman's name, given up."

The fat superintendent straightened up, stretched back in his chair, and laughed. "Oh, lordy . . . you bloody . . . mugs," he said. "The Boss has got that sixty thousand nicker . . . and all the doin's from the Magnificent and he's vanished with the ruddy lot . . . an' all you got is peanuts and — " he nearly choked with mirth, "you don't know who the hell he is . . . where he is . . . or where and how to find him and the nicker."

"It's a bloody lie. You ain't tricking us that way, copper."

"Is it? You don't believe that, suckers. Listen . . . " Jones dialled the telephone exchange. "Miss," he said, "this is Scotland Yard. I want an ex-Directory number NOT 0627. I've rung it twice and can't get any reply. Can you find out what is wrong with it?"

There was a wait of two minutes during which Jones switched the telephone to a microphone and speaker. Then, "Sorry, Scotland Yard," a voice said, "but *NOT 0627 has been given up.*"

Jones replaced the receiver, switched off the microphone, and gazed benevolently at the four men in front of him. "Lumme, what with protection, blackmail, and the bank van he must have damned near a hundred thousand nicker stashed away somewhere. An' you lot got nuthin, and you can't go on the dole cos you ain't never worked."

It was the smallest of the four, Billy the Dip, who expressed the feelings of the stricken quartet. '"The double crossin' — " he said. "I'll slit his — , — throat. We earned the — money."

"Gawd damn it, Billy, how you goin' ter do that?" Jones asked. "You don't know him from Adam, except that he's got a navel and Adam hadn't. All right, they're all yours, Ainslie." He stood up and waddled from the room.

* * *

"Well now, gentlemen, I'm afraid we'll have to hold you on your own confession that you've been engaged in protection, blackmail and highway robbery to the tune of something like £100,000. You *did* say that the Boss was a double-crosser, and that *you* had earned the money, didn't you? It's on tape, by the way, if you feel like denying it later." He indicated a microphone. "It's a bit hard, I know,

277

to lose the doings, but doubtless the Boss paid you well . . . "

"The — — was keeping the money until it were safe to . . . " Billy began.

"Shut your trap, you damned fool," Scotch broke out.

"That'll be on tape, too," Ainslie pointed out. They gave it up, and went off to the cells to await further inquiries.

23

AINSLIE had a weak case, and he knew it. In fact, he had no evidence at all beyond the four men's statement: and since they had not been warned before making it, he could not even use that. The idea of the confrontation had been Jones's, and that wily old scout had been working on his own, and the Doctor's, case. His strategy became plain when, next morning, he had Scotch to himself in the Interrogation Room. He greeted the man's entrance with, "Sit down, Scotch . . . have a dose of lung cancer," holding out a cigarette case. They lit up together.

"Now, you're in a hole, Scotch, and you don't deserve to be in one," he said, sympathetically — and the old humbug could be mournfully sympathetic when he liked. "You've got no boss, no cash, no hopes, and a bleeding murder charge looming up."

Scotch started. He stared incredulously. "*Murder*! What the hell are you talking about, Super?"

"As if you didn't know! Come off it, Scotch. You know bloody well that the gang outed Johnny de Frees, and the private eye who'd got too near to you all, and tried to do in that Worth jane in Spain who put the private eye on to you."

The result of this conclusion on Scotch Jock was staggering. He nearly fainted and began shaking all over as though he had the palsy. Jones rang the desk bell. To the answering constable he said: "Get me a brandy from the canteen — and quickly."

The brandy brought some relief to Scotch, and also some speech. "Look, Super," he said, "you ain't a bad bloke, and you've always been fair to me and the others. All right, I was the Boss's right hand and I'll stand for that, though you couldn't put us away on what you've got. You know damned well that's right. But murder. You ain't puttin' that on me. I wouldn't touch it — nor would the others. A bit o' taking money away from them as can afford it — yes. But not any killing."

"De Frees and Danny Taylor were killed, Scotch."

"Not by us, Super. We ain't that crazy."

"Then by whom?"

"The Boss. I reckon he's ditched us, and I ain't standing by him any more."

Jones felt a comfortable glow of satisfaction.

"What? Himself?"

"No. He wouldn't have the bloody guts."

"Then who?"

"You ever heard of a chap called Pineapple?"

Jones nodded. "Sicilian . . . Mafia . . . name of Ricardo?"

"That's him. The Boss got him and a couple of Eye-ties with him."

"Cor lumme. Just so's he could take over de Frees's manor. He could have put him out of business."

"Nao. That wasn't the reason."

"Then why, Scotch? Here, have another cigarette." The case was presented again. For two or three minutes Scotch puffed out smoke. He gazed at the window, thinking . . . thinking. Then he came to a decision. "Look, guv'nor. I'll say this for you. You're a straight guy, and I wouldn't say it of any other dick. Now, I ain't in that bank car snatch. I gotta alibi, and I don't want it public unless I has to. Now, if you can keep me out of this do, I'll tell you something about de Frees. And I'm the only one that knows it."

Jones thought it over. It was as near as damn-it to compounding a felony and that's a serious thing in a police officer. He came at last to a decision. "Tell me your alibi, Scotch, and if I can satisfy myself on it, and that you weren't in the bank business, then it's a deal."

"Right. Here's the alibi." He detailed it. "It's cast iron."

"Cor lumme, that's a bit of luck for you, Scotch, else you'd have been in the snatch. Now — de Frees."

Scotch Jock began to talk. "It was like this. I was the Boss's outside man, if you get me?" Jones nodded. "You reviewed the arrangements in the scripts of the jobs."

"Right. Well, one day the Boss gets me on the phone and tells me to pick up a letter at me post-box (and where that was I ain't telling)."

"Fair enough," Jones agreed.

"This 'ere letter says I'd agree that we all had had a good time with him, but it'd come to an end unless Johnny de Frees was out of the way. It said as how Johnny was putting the black on him cos he'd found out who he (the Boss) was . . . "

"And who was he?"

"Cut me throat if I tells a lie,"

Scotch said earnestly. "I don't know. So far as knowing him is concerned, we wouldn't recognise him if he spoke to us; we ain't never seen him. And only me has heard his voice."

"Good enough, Scotch. Go on."

"Cutting a long story short, Super, he offered me five thousand pounds in notes to 'out' Johnny, any way I liked. Gawd strike me pink! I calls up that number you knows about and says nothing doing. I ain't having no truck with killing. That were that, and I carried out instructions in the letter and burns it.

"Things were a bit cool between us after that, but a fortnight later he phones me again. Did I know any Italian in the murky way? I gives him the name of one, and the next I hears is that he's got in touch with Pineapple Ricardo and fixed him up for Johnny."

"Who was the Italian you knew?"

"I can tell you that, because he's back in Sicily. Chap named de Monti."

"The little chappie who used to show shopkeepers a knife and walk out with money?" asked Jones who knew most of the underworld figures over a quarter of a century.

"That's him. Next thing I hears is that Johnny is dead and buried. Monti told me he and Ricardo had got the nicker and Ricardo had cleared out back to Sicily and he (Monti) was going that day. He said he'd be a rich man in his country with Ricardo."

"And what about Danny Taylor?"

"There, Super, I can't help you. Dunno nothing about him: only it wasn't Ricardo or Monti, they'd vamoosed."

"Right, Scotch. I'll check your alibi myself, and if it holds . . . " He left the sentence unfinished.

Jones carried the news of the talk to Doctor Manson and Inspector Kenway. The Doctor listened without interruption to the end, then eyed the Fat Man cynically. "Say it, Fat Man," he invited.

"Say it? Say what, Doctor?"

"Say 'I told you so'. You have maintained that I was wrong not to get in with the gang adventures. Well, you were right in believing that the gang warfare and the killings were not divided." He bestowed a smile on the fat superintendent, and placed a hand on his shoulders. "You've solved the killings," he said, and said it with pleasure. "Now, what do we do?"

"Over Johnny de Frees, Doctor — nothing. They're awa' and we can't do anything about it, and you bet the Mafia within Sicily won't do anything except collect some of the blood money if we tell 'em about it. As for Danny Taylor, it's still open."

"Do you believe Scotch Jock's account?"

"I'll bank on it. He doesn't hold with murder but so long as the Boss was bringing in money, and he was not involved in the killing, he kept silent. Now Danny's was a separate murder, but with the same object — keeping secret the identity of the Boss. I been busy. What about that bank snatch?"

The security van which had disappeared completely and had been missing for twenty-four hours, had been found in the early afternoon following the attack. A delivery man going to park his small van heard knockings coming from a garage he knew to be empty in a yard at Archway, Highgate, and called a police officer. The door was forced and the van found, with the two men still bound and gagged inside. One of them said he had been kicking his heels on the floor for hours without being heard.

Their story was soon told. When the pseudo police officers had been locked in and the van had resumed its interrupted journey, they had produced guns and while one of them kept them under threat of shooting, the other bound, blindfolded and gagged them. They heard the money being transferred from the van, and heard the leader say to the driver, "You know where to go. The Boss will be in touch." Then, they were locked in the van again and driven off.

Could they recognise the police officers? Yes, they thought they could though they had only a brief glance in the darkened interior of the van before being blindfolded. Through a one-way window in the Interrogation Room they pointed fingers at two of the men arrested in the Nite Lite. Asked to look at Scotch Jock, they said they had not seen him, but he might have been one of the crew of the van.

Jones, keeping his promise, investigated, minutely, Scotch's alibi and found it held beyond doubt; and Scotch was set free from the hijacking charge.

"And the affair at the Magnificent?" Jones asked.

"We've no evidence against him, Fatty," Ainslie pointed out. "Only the 'okey-dokey' message on the answering service of the telephone in Notting Hill. He can say he only conveyed information given to him."

"Well, he's solved the chief murder for us," Jones said. "Chuck the bastard out."

The A.C. heard the news of the arrest and confirmation of the identity of the hi-jackers. This was as good as it went, *but there was still no trace of the sixty thousand pounds of the bank's money*, he pointed out.

The arrested men, incensed at the double-crossing by the Boss would have told, if they could, where the money was likely to be. Two, who went off in the car with it, said their orders were to drive to Finsbury Park, and leave the car inside the entrance to the cricket ground, walk into Endyman Road, where they would find a car to pick them up and drive them to the Nite Lite. It did. What happened to the car with the money, and who picked it up, they had no idea.

Mrs. Worth and Mary, now free from danger and without the unwanted child, the result of her miscarriage, came home and identified one of the arrested men as one of the pair who had threatened her in Benidorm. All three were charged with complicity in the hijacking, and were sent for trial.

24

SIX weeks passed by.
Insurance had been paid out on the stolen bank money.

And that was all.

Nothing on the murder of Danny Taylor.

Scotch Jock had left London for the safety of the Provinces. He was, he said, getting clear of the Boss, whoever he was, lest he might hear that he (Jock) had talked. The Italian police, contacted, said that without evidence, and not hearsay, there was nothing they could do about the Sicilian, Ricardo, who now owned a café, or da Monti, who had a share in it. They were, to all intents and purposes, honest tradespeople.

It was at this stage that, to adapt Tennyson, good luck threw her old shoe after; that luck which, without it, crime would prosper even more than it does: and that is plenty. Pay no attention to those pedagogues and moralists who preach, sanctimoniously, that crime doesn't pay. It is paying in Britain at the moment to the tune of more than £100,000,000 a year put into the pockets of professional crooks, robbers, confidence men and shoplifters.

The luck that came the way of Doctor Manson and his Yard colleagues had as its good fairy the manager of a bank in Kensington, who telephoned Scotland Yard and asked that a senior officer should come along and see him on a matter of great importance. Inspector Ainslie paid him a hurried visit.

Inside his private room, the manager produced a long list of numbers, one of which was underlined. "These are the numbers supplied of certain notes in that raid on the bank security van, Inspector," he said: and Ainslie nodded; he had sent them out to all banks but without much hope of any results.

"And?" he queried.

The manager passed over the marked list. "And this," he said, putting a five-pound note on the desk. Ainslie compared the note with the number underlined on the list, and then held it up to the light and examined it. "And how did it come into your possession, sir?" he asked.

"One of my tellers — a smart man and conscientious — received it." He tipped a lever on his intercom. "Ask Mr. Shelley if he can spare me a few moments?" he requested.

A tall, black-coated figure entered. "Ah, Shelley," the manager said, "Inspector Ainslie, of Scotland Yard, re that £5 note."

"How did it come to your notice, Mr. Shelley?" Ainslie asked.

"It was paid in by a messenger from Ellis & Company, the Kensington jewellers, sir."

"Sure of that? And how?"

"Quite sure, sir. The messenger came in just as we were closing the doors.

293

When I came to check up afterwards, his cheques and notes were on top of my drawer. I automatically noted the note's number and compared it with the Yard's list. Then I told the manager."

Mr. Frank Ellis, senior partner in the jewellery firm, agreed that he had taken the note with others, in payment for a diamond ornament. "But what is the trouble, Inspector?" he asked.

"Do you know from whom you received it, Mr. Ellis?"

"Certainly, from a very good but occasional customer." He mentioned a name. Ainslie sat very still for a moment. Then: "You are certain of that, Mr. Ellis?"

"Quite certain, sir. It was the only £5 note I had taken that day. Is there anything wrong with it?" he asked anxiously.

"With the note — no, sir. But I would be glad if you did not mention anything of this outside this room."

Ainslie hurried back to the Yard, and to the A.C. Sir Edward heard the incident sitting with Doctor Manson, Superintendent Jones and Chief Inspector Kenway, hurriedly called in.

"And who was the customer?" the A.C. asked, and was told.

The name produced something like consternation. The five men gazed unbelievingly into each others' eyes. Jones broke the silence. His astonishment was so great as to reduce his usual roar into a sibilant whisper. "Cor lumme," he said. "Cor lumme. We bin going round a ruddy mulberry bush . . . the Boss."

"Don't jump to conclusions, Jones," Doctor Manson cautioned. "It looks that way, but he may have received it from somebody."

Jones snorted. "It's more likely a ruddy mistake. They all make 'em at some time, even the cleverest of 'em. That's how we catch 'em."

"Well, Fat Man, let us with Crane 'glory in a great mistake', if it is, because this is a very great one." He thought for a moment. "Have we got a tame magistrate about the place?"

"Why?" the A.C. asked.

"Because I want an open search warrant — and I'll fill in the name and address."

"That's easy, Doctor," said Kenway. "He's a J.P.," pointing at the A.C. Doctor Manson eyed the C.I.D. chief, quizzingly.

"I don't like it," the A.C. said.

"We can't let it go outside, Edward. It's a pretty grave assumption, you know. And if he *is* the Boss then de Frees was killed by his orders. I'll go along myself with Jones and Ainslie — at night."

At midnight the three, with a safe expert entered an office on the first floor of a block in Gresham Street. Behind the shield of a dark blue blind they began a search of the two rooms which comprised the small suite. The desk and all cupboards and drawers were safely locked, but were easily opened. They contained letters and business documents of no interest to the searchers. "He seems to have had a genuine business connection," Manson said after going through them.

A top right-hand drawer inside the roll-top desk was also locked, and when opened was seen to contain only stamps.

Jones was regarding the desk with on his face the expression which usually got there when he was engaged in thought. He stirred into activity. "'Ere, let me have a dekko inside, Doctor," he said. "I know a bit about these desks." He fiddled about with the drawer, pulled it out and then fiddled with the interior. "Ah," he said — and his voice oozed with satisfaction. "I thought so. There's a back compartment." More fiddling and there was a sharp sound of sliding. Jones's hand went into the hidden compartment and came out with an article. He whistled, shrilly, and opened his hand. It held a small automatic. Together, they looked it over. "Belgian,

I think," the Doctor said. "A handbag weapon." He wrapped it carefully in a handkerchief and then enclosed it in a large brief envelope taken from the desk.

"We'll look over it in the lab," he explained.

The Yard's safe expert was lounging in one of the two arm-chairs in the office. "Were you wanting me for anything, Commander?" he asked. "There doesn't seem anything here in my line."

Doctor Manson gave a start. "No," he said, and looked round. "That's rather odd. There doesn't appear to be a safe in the place."

"Odd is an understatement," Ainslie said. "I've never known an office without a safe yet."

"Scout round," suggested Jones.

"We *have*, Fat Man," Ainslie protested. "There isn't anything. But we'll have another look for hidden objects."

There was no safe hidden behind

the various pictures on the walls — the usual 'hiding' place always looked for by thieves (!). Across the end of the room panelling ran from floor to ceiling, in the centre of which hung a picture of the Thames taken from Waterloo Bridge. Other walls were panelled only halfway up. The door of the office was also of panelled wood. Beading ran along the top and sides of the wall panelling. The search, the second, produced nothing.

The four were about to pack up and leave when the Doctor, glancing round to make certain that no trace was being left of their intrusion, and running his gaze over the floor, suddenly paused. For half a minute he continued staring at the floor, his brows creased and wrinkles in the corners of his eyes — sure sign to Yard men that something unaccountable was troubling him.

"Ainslie, and you, Jones, come over here by the door . . . Look over the floor round about the desk and the filing cabinet. What do you notice about the carpet?"

They looked, a little puzzled. "Nothing, Doctor — except that the pile shows signs of wear down where feet have gone to and fro. And you'd expect that, wouldn't you? The carpet is not exactly new."

"Quite. Now look carefully round and see if you can see similar wear, not quite so obvious, elsewhere in the carpet."

A minute or two of scrutiny passed. "No, I don't notice anything, Doctor," Ainslie said. Jones, who knew his Manson, dealt more warily. He was slow to apprehend things, but pugnacious and tenacious enough to worry over them. The eyes in his fat face wandered over the carpeted floor, and after several glances stayed near the panelled wall. He looked at his chief, inquiringly.

The Doctor smiled in appreciation. "And why, Jones, should there be an impression of passage ending in front of a panelled wall?"

"By God!" Jones said blasphemously.

From a pocket the doctor took a lens and through it inspected minutely the panelling. He examined every inch of the beading edging, and ran a finger along its height from knee level upwards. The action produced a slight whizzing sound and a section of the panelling, about six feet by three feet began to roll open. In the opening was revealed a large safe fully five feet high and two feet wide.

The doctor motioned the Yard safe expert forward. A couple of minutes' examination and he gave his verdict. "It will take me a good hour, I'm afraid, Doctor," he announced.

"Get busy, there's a good chap."

With a stethoscope taken from his bag, the expert knelt in front of the safe and turned slowly the combination wheel, listening through the stethoscope to the falling of the tumblers inside the lock. Now and again he tried the door, but without success. "It's a six letter combination, I think, sir," he said. The hour passed and another quarter after it, before he turned, caught the eyes of the forensic chief and nodded. Rising, he pulled on the door, which came slowly open. The four craned to look inside.

The interior of the safe was crammed with packets of bank notes, piled across the width and for some distance up from the floor.

Jones broke the stupefied silence. "Stone the ruddy crows," he burst out with a roar. "*The Boss's cache. Whatyer know?*"

For the space of moments they stared at the sight. Never see so much nicker in me life," Jones lamented. Kenway spoke almost incoherently: "Shall I get help and a van and remove it, Doctor?"

"No. Certainly not!" Manson turned to the safe expert. "Can you close it again and set a different six letter combination?"

"Sure, Doctor. I'll make it 'Manson'.

We can easily remember that." He grinned.

It was 3 a.m. when they finally left the office.

At six o'clock the same morning a man from the Ballistics Department of the Yard, having received the automatic found in the secret drawer of the raided office, descended to a basement in the Yard and fired two shots from it into a bale of wool. He extracted the bullets and took them back to Ballistics. There, under a comparison microscope he compared them with the bullet extracted from the body of Danny Taylor.

An hour later he telephoned Doctor Manson: "It's the gun that killed Taylor," he reported.

At ten-thirty Inspector Baxter, head of 'Prints' came to the laboratory. "You wanted me, Doctor?" he asked. Manson handed him photographs of the fingerprints brought up from the automatic, and a bundle of signed witness statements given to the police during their investigations.

"H'm! Any particular one in mind, Doctor?"

"You know me better than that, Baxter. I don't give leads. I want independent views."

"Right-O." Baxter bent over the statements. "You know, Doctor," he said, "I'm looking only for identical prints. It would take me hours to inspect and check all the pages which have been handled, and identify the prints made — including yours." The Doctor nodded. "Find them, Baxter, and then we'll see."

Prints were brought up on document after document, and one by one were scrutinised and discarded. With only three documents remaining, Doctor Manson, and Jones with him, showed signs of frustration.

Then: "Ah, here they are," Baxter announced, and passed over a witness's statement. Doctor Manson looked at the signature, and passed it over to Jones and Kenway. "Make them permanent, Baxter," he said, "and keep it safe."

He sat back in his chair. "We've been a little slow-witted, I'm afraid," he commented.

25

ELEVEN o'clock, and the traditional coffee hour in City offices. The commissionaire of a block of offices in Gresham Street, an ex-detective sergeant, telephoned Inspector Ainslie.

"He's settled in, sir," he said.

"Right, Marshall, we'll be along. Thanks."

The commissionaire knocked on the door of an office, and threw it open. "Chief Inspector Ainslie and Commander Manson of Scotland Yard to see you, sir," he announced.

"Ha! Come in," the occupant of the room said. "Good morning, Ainslie . . . Doctor. Have some coffee. I take it you have news for me at last."

"I have news, sir. Rather unfavourable, I'm afraid. I have a warrant for your arrest on a charge of conspiracy in connection with the recent robbery of sixty thousand pounds from a bank security van on Hampstead Heath . . . "

"What the devil nonsense are you talking, Inspector? Is this a joke? I have never been near Hampstead Heath, not for years . . . "

"I know you weren't there. You were collecting a car from inside the cricket ground at Finsbury Park. The car contained the money in bank containers. Incidentally, we have your men in custody; and very angry they are at being double-crossed in the matter of money. We have also listened to conversations in the room in Notting Hill, and have copies of the telephone answering service."

"This is incredible Inspector. Men! I have no men, as you call them. I . . . "

"Would you care to open your safe for us, sir?"

"Safe? Look round you, man. I have no safe."

Ainslie crossed to and opened the door, and beckoned to a waiting man.

307

"Come along in and get to work, Stevens," he said.

The safe expert crossed to the panelled wall and slipped the panel back. Using the combination 'Manson' he opened the safe. The office occupant sat as if mesmerised, staring.

"How do you account for all this money?" Ainslie asked. "By the way, there are other charges." He stepped aside making way for Doctor Manson.

"You know that I am the police officer concerned with homicide," the Doctor began. "I have here a warrant *charging you, Norman Worth*, with the murder of one, Daniel Taylor, at premises in Notting Hill."

Ainslie, watching the man closely, saw a nerve jumping in a cheekbone.

Manson, continuing, said: "And I have a second warrant charging you with conspiracy to murder one, Johnny de Frees, at the Saxon Hall Hotel. I have to warn you that you are not bound to say anything in reply to the charges, but should you make any statement it will be taken down in writing, and may be used in evidence."

"You must be mad, sir. You have gone fully into my alibi at the time of de Frees's death, and into my statements. I did not for a moment leave the hotel that night."

"I should tell you, Worth, that we know all about Ricardo and di Monti . . . "

"They never saw me," Worth said. A second later a hand flew to his mouth. He collapsed, knowing that the words had given him away beyond all retraction.

"Our information is that de Frees had identified you as the Boss of the protection racket in the West End . . . "

"The bastard deserved to die," Worth broke out in a passion. "A cheap Italian crook blackmailing me to marry my daughter and come in on my organisation. To marry my daughter . . . MY daughter."

"And the private eye, Worth?" Manson

queried. "In case you were thinking of prevaricating, I should tell you that we have the automatic that was concealed in the secret drawer of this desk."

Worth sank back in his chair. Saliva appeared in the corners of his mouth. They took him away.

Jones heard the story of the arrest. He shook his head. "A cheap Italian crook wanting to marry his daughter," he said. "Cor stone the flaming crows. Wasn't he a ruddy crook himself?"

Manson grinned. "There are stratas of crooks, Fat Man, as there are stratas of Society. And they don't integrate — either of them."

"There's one thing that's puzzling me, Doctor, about the de Frees business." Jones tucked his brows. "How come it that the Wops knew about de Frees bein' at Saxon Hall?"

"Easy, Fat Man. You remember that Worth was objecting to his daughter marrying or wanting to marry de Frees? Well, as a sop to his daughter, he, not she, invited de Frees to spend a day in their company for a 'friendly' discussion. They walked along the herbaceous border so that the Italians could get a glimpse of him. And they were waiting for him just beyond the drive gates of the hotel when he left. So Worth was apparently in the clear — "

"Except for the Doctor's ancient Saxon edict," Kenway said.

"And what's that?" Jones demanded.

"*Murdir woll out atte last.*"

THE END

Other titles in the
Linford Mystery Library:

A GENTEEL LITTLE MURDER
Philip Daniels

Gilbert had a long-cherished plan to murder his wife. When the polished Edward entered the scene Gilbert's attitude was suddenly changed.

DEATH AT THE WEDDING
Madelaine Duke

Dr. Norah North's search for a killer takes her from a wedding to a private hospital.

MURDER FIRST CLASS
Ron Ellis

Will Detective Chief Inspector Glass find the Post Office robbers before the Executioner gets to them?

A FOOT IN THE GRAVE
Bruce Marshall

About to be imprisoned and tortured in Buenos Aires, John Smith escapes. only to become involved in an aeroplane hijacking.

DEAD TROUBLE
Martin Carroll

Trespassing brought Jennifer Denning more than she bargained for. She was totally unprepared for the violence which was to lie in her path.

HOURS TO KILL
Ursula Curtiss

Margaret went to New Mexico to look after her sick sister's rented house and felt a sharp edge of fear when the absent landlady arrived.

THE DEATH OF ABBE DIDIER
Richard Grayson

Inspector Gautier of the Sûreté investigates three crimes which are strangely connected.

NIGHTMARE TIME
Hugh Pentecost

Have the missing major and his wife met with foul play somewhere in the Beaumont Hotel, or is their disappearance a carefully planned step in an act of treason?

BLOOD WILL OUT
Margaret Carr

Why was the manor house so oddly familiar to Elinor Howard? Who would have guessed that a Sunday School outing could lead to murder?